HARRIET

To Midge, my dear friend,
with love,
          Buly 30-09-03

HARRIET

ELIZABETH ARCHER NASH HILL

iUniverse, Inc.

New York Lincoln Shanghai

HARRIET

iUniverse, Inc.

For information address:
iUniverse, Inc.
2021 Pine Lake Road, Suite 100
Lincoln, NE 68512
www.iuniverse.com

ISBN: 0-595-28792-1

Printed in the United States of America

This book is dedicated to my mother, Ruby Richardson Archer, who also relocated to Great Pond, Maine because of a family illness. She possessed many of the virtues which Harriet Kenney, the inspiration for my novel, displayed. Her courage, determination and dedication to her family's quality of life mirrored my heroine's in many situations.

CONTENTS

▼

Preface

This book was inspired by my reading brief comments about my Great-Great Great-Grandmother, Harriet Kenney Williams' life in my Uncle Gleason's genealogy of the descendants of Joshua Williams.[1](See footnote page ix) I was both grateful and proud to be related to such a courageous and devoted woman, who traveled in an ox cart with her husband and four young children from New Brunswick, Canada through the wilderness to the tiny township of Great Pond, Maine (Then Plantation #33) to assist her husband, Simeon's parents, who because of ill health, needed their assistance.

I originally planned to write Harriet's biography, but it soon became apparent that insufficient factual information was available for me to accomplish this. Instead, I decided to utilize the references concerning this remarkable woman in my Uncle's genealogy to create a fictional character endowed with a few of her virtues, which I so greatly admired. These were her deep religious faith, courage, and dedication to the needs of her husband and his parents, as well as those of her own family. Although some of the actual given names of the people portrayed in this novel have been used, their surnames have been changed, and I have created several fictional characters. Harriet, Simeon, Joshua, Bethiah, and Elizabeth, as well as those of some of Harriet's children, are the persons whose given names have been utilized and their surnames have been changed. Although factually, Harriet bore ten children, I have portrayed characters of only six of them. Joshua Williams was actually one of the first settlers of Great Pond. (At that point,

---

1. Ancestors and Descendants of Joshua Williams, a Mayflower Descendant & Pioneer. Gleason L. Archer, LL.D, a Great-Great-Grandson. Boston. Wright & Potter Printing Co. 1927.

known as Plantation #33.) All the personages whom I have depicted throughout this book are completely fictional.

When I was two years old, my parents moved from Pelham, New Hampshire to return to Great Pond, Maine, my father's birthplace. I remained there, except for my four high school years in Bangor, Maine until I was eighteen, growing up in the old family homestead. Also, I resided in Maine until moving to Haverhill, Massachusetts in 1961. During my childhood, I frequently visited the family, who at that time owned and lived within the same walls of the house, which was located about a half mile from ours, where Harriet spent the remaining days of her life. She resided there with her oldest son, James, his son, Ezra, and his wife, Vienna (usually referred to as "Dana."), who were my Great Uncle and Great Aunt. When Aunt Dana later resided in Bangor, Maine, I visited her during the time when I was a student at Bangor High School. In retrospect, I wish that I had asked her the many questions I might have, because Harriet had been her mother-in-law, and she possessed a wealth of information concerning her life. I have attempted to be as accurate as possible when alluding to historical facts by consulting various books and other works, as well as internet resources.

CHAPTER 1

▼

THE JOURNEY

Trees, November stark, lined the narrow winding road through the forest. Harriet always saw beauty in every season. To her, the bare branches exposed just another element of their wonder, the lovely symmetry of their forms. Also, there were always the evergreens permeating the landscape, symbolizing eternal spring. But the darkening sky, promising a chilling rain or perhaps even snow, troubled her. She wrapped the wooly blanket more snugly around her two year old daughter, Jennie, who slept peacefully in her arms. Simeon Jr., three, was sleeping in the rear of the ox cart, nestled under a heavy wool quilt Harriet's mother gave her, just before their parting embrace. Both women knew their separation would be for a long time, but neither allowed herself tears, although mother and daughter were very close. "Soul-mates "was how they described their relationship, and Harriet was only twenty. So young, her mother mused, to go to such a primitive place. Simeon's mother had described it in detail in her letter which Simeon and Harriet that had shared with her:

September 30, 1821

My Dear Simeon,

What I must ask you to do pains me considerably. But ask I must. Pa is getting weaker by the day and needs you badly. His old war wound in his hip is very painful now and he has trouble getting around much. He doesn't complain. You know how he is, but I know how much he is suffering although he won't admit it. That is why I'm writing this without telling him. Don't let him know I asked you to come. He would be awfully upset. I can't seem to help him the way I used to either, and it bothers me a lot. Son, I know how hard it would be for you to come here, especially with a wife and babies. Unfortunately, Great Pond (We gave it the same name as that pond at the end of the road instead of calling it Plantation #33 anymore), hasn't changed much since you left. We still don't have a store closer than ten miles away and the nearest doctor is in Ellsworth. 32 miles is a long way if one is ailing bad.

We all still have log houses. Pa was hoping to get some clapboards on ours, since he got the mill running last year, but there's just been no time. It seems to take forever to clear the land. You know how rocky the soil is here. We're still digging gardens in around the trees with a hoe. Clearing pastureland and enough for the hay fields is more of a priority.

Don't have a school or church yet either. We take turns meeting at one another's houses for prayers, Bible reading, and hymn singing. There's only ten families here now, and they teach their little ones letters and ciphering at home. So sadly enough, this place doesn't have much to offer in comfort or culture for your dear wife. It's a shame, because she's so young and bright.

Again, my dear Son, I apologize for asking so much of you and your little family—to give up your land, comfortable house, your cobbler shop, and all the other sacrifices this move would bring. If you feel that you can't come, just let me know, and I'll understand. It's an awful lot to ask of you and Harriet, especially at this time of the year.

Heaps of love & kisses to all,
Your loving Mother

Elizabeth's heart turned leaden, picturing her daughter in the family way again, jostling along in an ox cart for over 100 miles, and then bearing labor pains in such a primitive place with medical assistance so far away. What if something went wrong during the birthing? But Harriet had married her dashing "Yankee lover" with his dark wavy hair and the bluest eyes she had ever seen when she was only sixteen, and after reading about Harriet's in-laws' plight, Elizabeth knew that her daughter would willingly join her husband if he decided to go. Simeon had come to her native New Brunswick to seek his fortune, having tired of attempting to eek out a living in the tiny Maine settlement of Plantation #33 where he and his young family were now returning to assist his ailing parents.

Harriet brushed a stray lock of hair from her face and hurriedly dabbed an escaped tear from her deep brown eyes. The reality of leaving her family, friends, and everything familiar to her for this new home in the wilderness surged through her small frame like a turbulent wind battering a foundering ship. She leaned her face into the warmth of Jennie's blanket hiding her face, while suppressing her tears. Harriet forced herself to smile bravely and attempted to fix her thoughts upon Ruth, whom she had read about in the Old Testament. She was a young widow, who had courageously left her people in Moab to join her mother-in-law, Naomi, in her journey to her former home in Judah after losing both her son and her husband. Since her other daughter-in-law had reluctantly decided to return to Moab, Naomi pleaded with Ruth to join her, but the young woman replied, "Entreat me not to leave thee, or to return from following after thee, for whither thou goest, I will go; and where thou lodgest, I will lodge. Thy people will be my people, and thy God, my God."

How Ruth must have loved her husband and how devoted she was to her mother-in-law. Harriet mused, and unlike that poor girl, I still have my beloved Simeon and his mother needs me, just as Ruth's husband's mother did. After this comparison, Harriet sensed a peace permeating her being, similar to the kind she had felt after basking in the lovely hues of a rainbow following a thunderstorm.

As if he had sensed her thoughts, Simeon took her hand, kissing it gently, his face radiant with love. Harriet nestled close to him and resolved to face these changes in her life with God's help, cheerfully and bravely, realizing how difficult it must be for her dear husband as well. Leaving the thriving cobbler's shop he had worked so diligently to establish and the snug little home he had lovingly built with such wonderful craftsmanship for his little family, must be extremely painful for him. Early in the couples relationship, Simeon had told her how discouraged he had become with waiting for more people to arrive to assist in settling the tiny township he had left and this had led to his emigrating to New Brunswick Even after he had begged his father to join him, Joshua wished to remain in the tiny hamlet, holding fast to his belief that soon other families would be attracted to settle there because of the offers of generous land grants. Harriet sighed deeply, while contemplating her future in such an isolated place. Then suddenly she remembered reading that on March 15, 1820, which was the previous year, Maine had separated from Massachusetts to become a state, offering settlers a chance to have exciting new opportunities and challenges. Perhaps that will encourage more people to come here, she reasoned, feeling comforted by this possibility.

Now with ten more miles to go, the sky fulfilled its promise, pelting heavy droplets of rain against the canvas covered frame Simeon had built for the ox cart to protect his family from the elements. Harriet hugged her baby closer, thankful that her husband had planned for their comfort on the long journey.

"Harriet, I'm going to pull over beneath those pines, to get us and the oxen out of this rain for a little while. It's coming down hard and that grove will offer a little protection. We all need a rest and so do those hard working beasts."

This was one of the many things Harriet appreciated about Simeon. He was not only considerate of her and their children, but of animals as well, no matter how exhausted he might be himself. Now his eyes were clouded with concern. She knew he worried that the rain might soon become icy needles or heavy snow, and they had ten miles yet to cover. Oxen could only travel about 15 miles a day. Simeon had chosen them over horses, which were faster, because of their superior endurance and strength. It was cozy in the little cluster of evergreens and Harriet felt protected and snug, as though she were in sheltering arms. Trees always made her feel that way, even though occasionally she had heard a faint rustling in the bushes which lined the road, a former Indian trail. Other times she sensed a presence. Probably some curious animal, Harriet reasoned, or perhaps an Indian. Simeon had told her that the Indians in this area had been friendly and helpful to the settlers, so she wasn't concerned about their safety if one of them happened to be nearby. Feeling drowsy, Harriet leaned contentedly against his shoulder, completely unaware of the tall, lean young man seated upon an Indian pony, who had followed the travelers as close to the trail road as he dared without risking being noticed. His red-gold hair was almost the same shade as that of the beautiful young woman bouncing along in the ox cart. Although his name was Jonathan, he was called Gold Fox, by the Indians who had rescued and raised him since his parents were killed during the war of 1812. The name Gold Fox had been chosen for him because of the color of his hair. They had discovered him huddled in a charred room which was all that remained of his family home, terrified and half starved. Gold Fox had seen few white women since his adoption at age twelve. He was shy and didn't wish to reveal himself, even when he spotted the catamount, an especially dangerous wild cat, crouched in a tree dangerously near the backs of the oxen. His arrow had been true to his aim, brushing the top of the animal's head and startling it just enough to jump from the tree and to dart into the woods. Gold Fox found it difficult to kill animals, akin to the feelings of his Indian friends, who had taught him just as they had their young braves, that animals were only to be killed for meat and their hides or when attacked by one of them. Of course if his ruse hadn't worked, he would have done so with one whiz of his arrow. After the incident, despite the storm, he followed the small party until they reached the settlement beyond the forest. Resembling a walking snowman, Jonathan managed to find a small cave where he and his exhausted pony spent the night. After the blizzard abated, he made his way through the snow, and while returning to the Indian camp, experienced a loneliness unfamiliar to this young man of 20 summers.

When the weary travelers finally reached their destination, the storm had developed into a full scale blizzard, and Joshua and Bethiah's log house looked like a palace. Simmering in a large kettle hung over a blazing fire in the red brick fireplace, sat a rich, meat stew. Harriet had smelled nothing more delicious in her entire life. After hugs of welcome, Bethiah served the ravenous young family heaping portions of her delicious, hot soup in bowls from the set of china she had brought from her former Taunton home. When she noticed her petite daughter-in-law, who looked so young and vulnerable, still shivering from her long, cold journey, she draped her shoulders with one of her own cozy shawls. Why she looks little more than a child herself and already the mother of two babies, she mused, and by the tell tale swelling below the girl's waist, another was on its way. Oh dear, I would have waited to ask them to come if I had only known! But Bethiah's seasoned midwife's eye noted that her daughter-in-law appeared to have weathered the journey well and already appeared to be more rested and relaxed now that she was in a warm house, and had a nice hot meal. This helped assuage the instant guilt she felt, when finding that Harriet was pregnant. Then she gently brushed her daughter-in-law's hair with a kiss. After that motherly gesture, Harriet shut her eyes tightly to avoid tears, while picturing the mother she had left behind. It was the first time that they would live such a long distance apart from one another. When leaving home after her marriage to Simeon, the couple's house had been only five miles from her family homestead. When reflecting upon Bethiah's loving gesture, Harriet sensed that her mother-in-law would be not only a friend but a mother figure as well.

After the children were snuggled cozily in a bunk, covered with a warm, wool quilt Bethiah had made by utilizing pieces gleaned from Joshua's worn out shirts and coats, and Simeon bedded down the weary oxen in the log barn, they all sat around the fire, whose orange-red flames pranced over maple logs, drinking hot tea, brewed deep red in color just the way Harriet liked it. As exhausted as they all were, their visiting kept them up far into the night. Although married five years, this was the first time Harriet had met her husband's parents. Their only acquaintance had been through letters.

Harriet was startled to see how frail Bethiah and Joshua were. They were handsome people though. It was easy to see why her husband was so attractive; his features were as finely etched as theirs were, and Harriet considered him the handsomest man she had ever met. Bethiah must have been a beauty in her day. Her delicate features, with only tiny lines like those of well worn porcelain, despite years of hard work, still gave her a fragile loveliness. Although Joshua moved slowly because of a a wound in his hip incurred during the Revolutionary war which became increasingly painful as he grew older, his dark hair, flecked with silver was abundant and his face sustained a hint of youth, despite lines etched by suffering and advancing age. How badly they needed us, Harriet mused, while observing their fatigue as the couple walked toward their bedroom.

Harriet was surprised to find three bedrooms, a loft, large kitchen and living room in the house which seemed so small, when she had observed it from the road. Outside, wind howled like a giant who had been imprisoned and now free, was venting his rage on whatever stood in its path by pounding the shingled roof with hail stones and beating against the plank door with a heavy fist. If the young family had been only an hour later they would have experienced the full force of the raging storm.

CHAPTER 2

▼

A NEW ARRIVAL

The morning dawned, peaceful and unusually warm. It is the New England weather living up to its fickle reputation just as Simeon had described, Harriet observed. It was though nature had regretted its rampage and wishing to atone for it, opened a cache of diamonds, sprinkling them to glitter on the tips of the maples and pines. She stood at the window basking in the beautiful panorama outside until someone hammered frantically on the front door.

Bethiah rushed to the door in a manner not expected from one almost seventy, as though she expected the young man whose voice came in gasps from running, while he said, "It's Amy's time! The baby's coming!" Watching how quickly she calmed the distraught expectant father, Harriet realized that her mother-in-law had had considerable experience in calming many men in this bewildered state, and that she must be the tiny hamlet's midwife. Quickly Bethiah assembled clean linens, herbs for tea, a jug of soup, donned her shawl and headed for the door. Then hesitating, she turned toward Harriet saying, "I don't like to ask this of you, Harriet, dear, with you being so exhausted from your travels, but I'd like to have you come with me. Grandpa and Simeon can watch the babies."

"Of course, Mother Wilson, I'm quite rested and I'd like to come and help in any way I can," responded Harriet, wondering if Bethiah wanted her to learn the art of midwifery, in case there was no one else to attend to these women so far from doctors, when she was unable to perform this service herself. While Simeon hitched up Joshua's buckboard for the ten mile ride to Benjamin Moore's cabin, Bethiah murmured, "My Dear, I didn't want Ben to hear this, but Amy must be having a hard time. I'm afraid it may be a breach birth, and I'll need your help in trying to turn the baby. With your small hands, so much stronger than my arthritic ones, it might be possible."

For a moment, Harriet hesitated. What a responsibility! The only births she had witnessed were her own. But trusting in the expertise of Bethiah, and after murmuring a quick prayer, she managed what she hoped was a confident smile and said, "I'll do my best."

When they arrived, Harriet fought back tears of compassion for the girl writhing with pain, whose dark hair, drenched with perspiration, fell in wet strands around her small, childlike face. Amy clutched her terrified husband's hand while he looked at her helplessly. Bethiah immediately took charge of the situation, sending Ben to rekindle the neglected fire and to fetch water to heat. Amy, diverted momentarily from her pain by Harriet's presence, asked her if she had any babies. "Two," replied Harriet. Attempting to keep her voice reassuring she said, "I know how it hurts now, but in a little while, you will be holding your precious baby, and will be happier than you ever dreamed you could be." Then she gently touched the girl's distended abdomen, wishing that somehow she could snatch away the agony which tore through the young woman's body. Harriet's childbirths had been comparatively easy, but then her mother was there for encouragement and comfort. Also, her babies had come without any complications during their births.

After what seemed an eternity, Bethiah and Harriet managed to turn the baby, and deliver the lusty voiced son into the arms of his exhausted, but delighted mother. After heating the jar of soup Bethiah brought for the relieved and happy father, and bringing some tea and toast to Amy, their mission was accomplished. Harriet marveled at the skill of her mother-in-law, and murmured thanks for her answered prayer. After Bethiah was certain that the young mother had recovered sufficiently to be left in her husband's care, She and Harriet changed the bed with clean, lavender scented sheets, which they had brought with them and tucked the young woman in her bed to rest after her ordeal. With Harriet's help, Bethiah gathered up the worn, soiled linens along with whatever other laundry needed to be done to take home to wash. Then her lips brushed the tiny cheek of the newborn while she placed him in the cozy cradle, which Joshua had constructed as a present for the baby, covering him with the warm blankets Amy had made.

Touching Bethiah's hand gently, Amy said, "I can't begin to thank you enough for all you have done for me, and you too, Harriet. You are both so loving and caring. I will wash and return these lovely scented sheets as soon as I can."

"That's what neighbors are for, and the sheets are a gift for you. The cradle is the baby's present, and I thought it would be nice for his mother to have a little gift as well. Now go to sleep, Child, you need your rest. I'll show Ben how to hold the baby before I leave and have him practice a little so he will feel a little more at ease with him. New fathers tend to be a little nervous about holding newborns."

After Harriet and Bethiah were certain that Ben would be comfortable enough to attend to the baby while Amy slept, they left for home. Later they would bring prepared food for the couple's supper. Along with the other neighbors, more meals would be brought until Amy was strong enough to cook herself. Also, all the women living nearby, would help with the cleaning and assist the new young mother in whatever ways they were needed. Harriet smiled, realizing that her new neighbors were much the same as the ones she had left behind in her former home in New Brunswick. It gave her a warm, cozy feeling. She was beginning to feel increasingly more at home. Impulsively, she hugged her mother-in-law, saying, "You are wonderful, Mother Wilson! Not only did you save that baby and probably Amy's life as well, but also you are so kind and thoughtful."

"Thank you, Child," Bethiah replied, "I was just being neighborly, and concerning the birthing, I had some help. My prayers were answered. Also, I am proud of my Daughter. You were a great deal of help, My Dear."

"I'm so happy that I could be of assistance," answered Harriet while the women climbed into the buckboard, sinking their tired bodies against its cushioned seats. Bethiah had made its cushions while sitting by the fire during the frigid winter evenings the previous year.

Six months later, Bethiah delivered Harriet's third child. She had been conscience stricken when she discovered that Harriet was carrying a child during her arduous journey from New Brunswick, and was doubly grateful when Elizabeth, a healthy, lively baby, was born after a relatively short labor, with little pain. Her tiny face framed with small tufts of feathery, dark hair, resembled that of Harriet's beloved mother, whose second granddaughter now was her first namesake. She immediately requested paper and pen to tell her the joyful news.

Relief surged through Elizabeth such as that one feels after the sun slides through, gilding snow covered branches after a violent blizzard, when she recognized the familiar handwriting on the letter she clutched in her trembling hands. Tears of relief spattered its pages while she murmured a quick prayer of thanks for Harriet's safe childbirth. She smiled, her face illuminating with love, picturing her daughter and her new grandchild, her beloved namesake. Quickly she went inside to share her happy news with Harriet's sister Betsey, and her brothers Charles, Henry, and Samuel. Along with their mother, they had worried about their sister and her pregnancy in such a primitive place. They all had spent many hours praying for Harriet's safe delivery, and now they dropped to their knees, clasped hands, and whispered prayers of thanks.

CHAPTER 3

▼

SETTLING IN

Harriet both admired and was amazed by the courage of her husband's parents. Joshua was a wounded veteran and already 60 when he came to settle this remote place, which was covered with dense forests and rocky terrain. How difficult it must have been for fifty nine year old Bethiah to leave her comfortable home in Taunton, Massachusetts when she accompanied him into the wilderness. It seemed almost impossible to Harriet that after only ten years, Joshua had cleared several acres of pasture land, built a house and barn, and planted crops. While her husband built their home, Bethiah had assisted him by gathering and matching rocks which they utilized for the foundation of their snug, little home. She had stood outside many evenings with a lantern long after the sun had dipped beneath the edge of the darkening forest which bordered their hard won pasture land, to provide light for his construction of their new dwelling place. While standing there, she worried because Joshua had already toiled twelve hours throughout the day clearing land and hoeing up patches of land to plant corn, turnips, beans, cabbages, beets and carrots, as well as rye, barley, wheat and pota-toes. He was constantly cutting dense brush and felling enormous trees with his axe to increase grazing space for their animals. The trees were needed for both buildings and firewood, so some of his work served a dual purpose which was comforting to her.

Harriet had never asked Simeon why this couple, so long past their youth, had left a comfortable home in Taunton, Massachusetts where Joshua had owned a grist mill, which had grown into a thriving business and provided much more appropriate work for a man with a wound in his hip, than the settling of such an isolated wilderness. Perhaps the move had been made because of the region's heavy timber, which could be sold for shipbuilding, as well as housing and so many other building projects, or the land grant of 150 acres, which Simeon mentioned the couple had received. Also, they might have hoped that the area would be remote enough to provide some peaceful surroundings. This would certainly be a welcome change from having lived through the many wars which had devastated the young country. There had been the King Georges War in 1745, which ended when Joshua was two years old in 1749, the Seven Years War from 1756-1763, the Revolutionary War in 1775, and the war of 1812. How they must have longed for a tranquil setting such as this little hamlet provided to spend their waning years But also, what Harriet had observed about her in-laws in the few months since she had arrived, their main motive appeared to have been the spirit of adventure. Hadn't she felt it deep within the forest, despite her reluctance to leave home, while the ox cart lumbered through the wilderness to reach their destination? She also, had left a comfortable home and an active social life, but she was only 20, she reasoned.

Harriet sometimes dreamed of the snug little house in Fredericton which Simeon had built, and where he had brought her as a bride. Simeon Jr. and Jennie had been born there, and she had felt so fortunate to have her own little household to manage. Sometimes she would awaken and gaze sleepily at the interior of the bedroom in her new home with Simeon's parents when momentarily, a twinge of homesickness would surge through her psyche. Then she would drift peacefully back to sleep. The next morning, while recalling the dream, she realized that she was becoming quite content in her new home. Also, Bethiah provided Harriet with a great deal of help with the children, which enabled her to have some much appreciated leisure time. She also realized how much her young daughter-in-law enjoyed going outside to bask in the wonders of nature.

After the weekly laundry had been washed as well as hung out to dry in the gentle spring breezes, a pot of beans placed in the oven to simmer for the evening meal, and bread dough prepared and placed in a covered bowl to rise, Bethiah finally convinced Harriet to indulge herself in some leisure, while the children napped. A little reluctantly, because there was yet so much work to do that day, she gratefully slipped outside, deeply touched by her mother-in-law's concern and her understanding of her need for some rest and a little time just for herself.

It had been an usually cold winter and finally spring had come, and somehow the grass and foliage, as well as the buds bursting into bloom seemed more abundant then in previous years, as if to recompense for the long, harsh winter. Harriet loved to sit in the sun, whether nestled on the cushioned seat which Simeon had built for her in the large, front parlor window, or on a moss covered rock by the brook. Sometimes she simply lounged on the grass or new mown hay. Its caressing rays gave her a feeling of well being, and she absorbed them like a flower raising its face to the sun's benevolent touch. Her invigorated spirit attuned to the quiet stirrings of the earth, along with the birdsong and gentle footfalls of tiny animals. During these times, she immersed herself so deeply in the earth's rhythm, that afterwards she translated them into melodies on her clavichord or memory paintings with her watercolors. Somehow, after these quiet times, her brush flowed as though it had a soul of its own into the essences of flowers, the wild roses tumbling over the rock pile on the edge of the orchard or the quiet misted mountains beyond the forest to endow her paintings with an almost mystical touch. These watercolors were the most representative of the creative impulses which surged through her being during these periods of profound tranquility and solitude. Also, during this total immersion in the splendor of nature was when she felt the closest to God, basking in the beauty of his creation—more precious and lovelier than any jewel or man-made object could ever be.

CHAPTER 4

▼

CHALLENGES

Not even a tablespoon of flour remained in either the corn meal or flour barrels. Harriet wearily pushed a strand of stray hair away from her eyes, heavy with unshed tears. With Simeon away in the deep forests, and both Bethiah and Joshua sick with bad colds and nothing to make bread with, Harriet felt as though all the mountains rising mauve and hazy above the trees bordering the pasture below, were resting firmly on her shoulders. The family larder contained five wizened potatoes, a few carrots, two beets, a bunch of onions, and a meager supply of salted meat. How can I find some way of obtaining funds to replenish it, she pondered? It would be six weeks before Simeon's return from the deep woods, where he was scaling lumber for another landowner, in order to provide some cash for his family's needs. Joshua's failing health, which made it impossible for him to be of much assistance in the cultivating of crops, had left Simeon, who had undertaken every odd job he could find to earn enough money to purchase another horse to replace the one who died, as well as two cows, and three hogs, had been left with little time for the planting and tending gardens. Also, the extreme cold of the previous winter had contributed to the diminished crops of vegetables, oats, corn, rye, and potatoes. The scanty harvest was not only insufficient for family needs, but also provided no surplus to sell for income they had counted upon to supply their staples and other needs for the coming winter.

I shouldn't have relied so much on Aunt Sarah's birthday gift to use for replenishing our food supply, Harriet agonized. She had torn the envelope open eagerly, but instead of the usual cash, it contained warm greetings and the promise of a parcel in the future. Harriet flushed with guilt, while remembering her disappointment. What could be happening to her? Was she succumbing to material needs, instead of those of the spirit? But money would have helped so much, because food was a necessity, she reasoned.

Because of the number of families who were not able to pay their bills because of the same shortage of produce which plagued Simeon's family, the Mosbys had been forced to deny any additional credit to their customers, so Harriet did not even have that option. With no money forthcoming from Simeon's wages until spring, she realized that there was only one way to raise the needed cash. Sell the brooch. The lovely family heirloom—a sparkling circle of diamonds surrounding a shimmering emerald. It had belonged to Grandmother Ellen and had been a gift from Grandpa Nathan when the couple became engaged to marry. Harriet's mother had pressed the brooch into her hand moments before Harriet left with her husband and family for Maine. Harriet wore the brooch often because it provided a link with home, and Matilda Mosby had always admired it, commenting on its beauty many times. She would be more than eager to take it in exchange for food supplies. Having made the decision, Harriet quite uncharacteristically darted outside, and threw her arms around the sturdy trunk of a weather-beaten oak, clinging to it as though it were an anchor to sustain her sea of tears. Its winter gaunt branches, groaned in a sudden gust of frigid air, as if to share Harriet's anguish.

"It is too much. It is the only tie with home I have," she sobbed. The thought of the family she had left behind and the comfortable living she shared with Simeon in their Fredericton home, caused her fountain of tears to overflow like the breaking of a dam, running down the gnarled bark of the tree. Finally aware that she couldn't allow herself to catch cold standing coatless in January winds, she dried her face on her apron, went inside and asked Bethiah to watch the children while she performed an errand. Thankfully, they were napping, so wouldn't require much attention from their grandmother, who was still feeling ill from her cold. Resolutely, she unpinned her beloved brooch from her dress. Although engulfed with memories of its former owner, she gently placed it in its velvet-lined box, wrapped it with a handkerchief, and placed it in her coat pocket. Well, at least there is a store in this tiny village, and I guess I should be grateful to have something to barter with so my family won't starve, she mused. When climbing into the ox cart to perform her sad errand, she managed a brave smile, because her mother had always told her that if one smiled, it helped lift clouds of sadness.

As Harriet entered the store, Matilda, a tall, large-boned woman, with expressive gray eyes and upswept brown hair, was rearranging shelves. While listening to her offer to exchange the brooch for food supplies, Matilda sensed the pride in this young woman's bearing, so she attempted to keep from expressing the compassion she felt for her. Harriet's soft brown eyes mirrored her sadness in parting with the brooch, despite her gallant attempts to mask her feelings. Matilda, also, had moved to this tiny township to follow her husband. Harriet came because of the declining health of her husband's parents, but Matilda was there because of her husband Albert's dream of starting a good-sized country store in this isolated place, and his seizing the opportunity to start a business where he believed that the population should be expanding rapidly, because of its rich forest, abundant wildlife, four ponds, and a river, not to mention the generous land grants given to encourage settlers. The move from Bangor had been difficult and with much sacrifice on Matilda's part, but Albert was her husband and she loved him.

To Matilda, the brooch was not only an impressive ornament, but it also represented dressing for concerts, lectures and all the cultural events Bangor provided. For a moment, her own eyes were almost filled with tears. Hastily, she fought off her homesickness, and concentrated on the girl who was trying to barter what must have been a much loved family heirloom for the necessities of life.

Knowing instinctively that Harriet would not accept charity, Matilda provided her with a generous supply of food and staples, including sacks of corn meal, rye and buckwheat flour, rice, dried beans, potatoes, onions, and carrots, as well as a generous portion of dried beef and salted codfish. Because of her reluctance to accept something so precious to the person who was bartering it for sustenance for her family, Matilda consoled herself with resolving to find a way to return the brooch as soon as possible, hopefully without offending its proud owner. Also, she pondered, the lovely ornament must have reminded Harriet of intellectual pursuits in New Brunswick, which fed something deep within her with another type of sustenance, just as those of Bangor had done for her. She sighed and reluctantly took the jewel from Harriet's extended hand.

Later when she told Albert about the incident, although she had assured him that she was reluctant to accept the brooch as payment for the groceries Harriet received, he was upset with her because she had done so.

"Matilda, how could you take that poor woman's brooch for payment," he had said, "It looks like something that must have been in the family for years. She must have hated to part with it."

"But she did not even ask for credit, and you said we couldn't afford to give it anyway," Matilda responded defensively.

After all, he had not seen the pride and determination in the young woman's face. It was the first time they had disagreed about anything, during the eight years of their married life and sudden tears stung her eyelids. Albert quickly took her in his arms and gently wiped them away with his big white handkerchief, holding her until her sobs subsided, murmuring, "You are right, Dearest, that is what I said about extending credit at this time, but I guess putting a policy like that into practice when someone is in need is not something I had not put enough thought into."

Yet his feelings about the matter only reinforced Matilda's feelings of sadness because she had accepted the brooch, and she was determined to find a way to return it at the earliest opportunity.

CHAPTER 5

▼

A NEW FRIEND

Every morning without fail for the past two weeks, Matilda had awakened with a queasy feeling in the pit of her stomach. The first time she had experienced it was the morning after the incident which had occurred concerning the brooch Harriet had traded for food. It had been Albert and Matilda's first quarrel, and his complete disapproval of her acceptance of Harriet's family heirloom, coupled with her own prickling conscience, she reasoned, must have caused her stomach upset. Also, she adored her husband and it saddened her to upset him in any way. Albert's warm, loving nature had swept her off her feet almost immediately after they first met. Her father had shown her little affection, and the only person who had given her any loving concern during her childhood was a governess who left to marry just after Matilda had felt that at last, someone made her feel worthy of being loved. Albert had given her the only real love she had ever experienced. However, it was now six weeks later, and the nausea continued.

After an examination by Bethiah, the experienced midwife told Matilda that she was with child. Matilda's reactions were mixed. Although she was ecstatic about finally becoming pregnant after eight years of marriage, and having almost given up hope of ever conceiving a child, somewhere in the darkened corridors of her being, lingered her old fear of dying in childbirth as her mother had done while bearing her. Perhaps that was why Papa had disowned her so easily when she refused to marry the pompous, notoriously wealthy lumber baron he had chosen for her. Instead, Matilda married Albert, a young grocer of modest means, who nurtured a dream of providing a little wilderness township with a good general store. Because of her mother's tragic death during her birth, her father, although perhaps not having been aware of it, had probably inadvertently held his innocent child responsible. Also, Matilda had overheard him voice his disappointment that she had not been the son he had yearned for when speaking to one of his business associates. As if she had any control over that! She pondered. However as a child, she agonized not only because of the loss of the mother, whose loving embrace she had never experienced, but also her feelings about her own life having been the cause of her death. As she matured, these feelings abated somewhat, but never completely. How she had longed for her father's affection throughout the years. Matilda had attended the finest schools, been exposed to the best culture Bangor offered, and had been provided with the most expensive clothing as well as whatever material things she desired. However, all the luxuries her father bestowed upon her did not mean as much as a loving hug would have. Nevertheless, she longed for him to be proud of her, and to be eagerly awaiting the birth of his grandchild, just as Bethiah and Joshua held out loving arms to greet each newly arrived baby of Harriet and Simeon's.

When Matilda tidied up the shelves in the store that morning, her thoughts returned to her dilemma concerning finding a way to return the brooch without hurting Harriet's pride. I'm having all I can do to work in the store these mornings, let alone being by myself when Albert has to make his trips to Bangor for supplies. Then suddenly she realized that one problem was the solution of the other. She would ask Harriet to fill in for her as needed in the store. She was bright and would learn whatever skills needed for her duties there, and probably Bethiah could watch the children while Harriet worked. The brooch could be returned in exchange for a portion of Harriet's wages. Smiling and feeling a weight as heavy as a knapsack filled with rocks slide off her shoulders, Matilda hitched up the buggy and headed for Harriet's.

CHAPTER 6

▼

HOMECOMING

When Simeon returned from the woods on an unseasonably warm day for April, he was amazed to find that there had been enough food to last the family during the long, cold winter. Harriet was reluctant to tell him about her arrangement with Matilda, which had given her the opportunity to replenish the family food supply, because he would be concerned that her work at home already kept her too busy to take on any additional work. Nevertheless, she had been forced to do so, after Bethiah had mentioned something about her working at the store. Simeon was appalled to see that his hard working young wife had taken on yet another duty, and that he hadn't somehow provided better for them before leaving to labor in the woods. However, Simeon was proud of Harriet for discovering a way to obtain provisions for their family.

How wonderful it felt to be home at last! He mused. Although his workday as a farmer was from early morning until dusk, his employment as a logger consisted of at least twelve to fourteen hours each day in the bitter cold. At night instead of a cozy home, he returned to a drafty cabin not much warmer than outdoors. The structure was made of logs with a shingled roof and the only heat provided was from a fire in the pit. Its smoke escaped from an opening in the roof which was designed for this purpose. During storms, snow drifted through the opening, sometimes almost extinguishing the fire, and the wind howled like a hungry giant seeking its prey. The men huddled together in crude bunks covered with boughs, which served as mattresses, shivering under their common quilt constructed of several pieces of wool cloth sewn together, with a filling composed of three thin blankets and a flannel backing. Their meals usually consisted of baked beans, salt pork, biscuits and hot tea, except for an occasional variation when they were served salted fish boiled with salt pork, or someone provided the cook with venison or some other game. Wet boots and socks were hung up near the fire to dry, and usually their brief time for relaxation during the evenings consisted of reading whatever outdated newspapers or magazines were available, and some of the men played a few games of cards or checkers. The air was permeated with the odor of unwashed bodies and smelly boots. The temperature inside was not conducive to bathing and although Simeon attempted to wash up a bit, there were few opportunities for good hygiene. However, the aroma of the evergreens covering the beds provided a occasional whiff of fragrance. Also, beans simmering in the pot, as well as the pleasant scent of biscuits baking in the cook shack, were a welcome respite from the unpleasant smells.

Simeon, along with scaling the lumber, also worked with the other men felling trees, and loading the heavy logs onto the sleds drawn by horses. These heavily laden vehicles were then hauled through the forest until they reached the river where the logging drive would take place. Proceeding through the slippery, icy snow in this manner was a dangerous task for the men as well as the horses. Also, the logging drive was extremely precarious, especially when a log jam occurred. Men wearing spiked boots jumped from one log to another, attempting to loosen entangled groups of logs, and if their balance were lost, it usually resulted in the loss of lives. After these unfortunate accidents, the men pooled together, each dropping some money in a sock or hat for the widows of those victimized in this hazardous duty. After reflecting upon a winter spent in the forest, especially under those circumstances, when Simeon climbed into bed with its lavender scented sheets beside his dear wife, he felt as if home were almost like a little foretaste of Heaven.

CHAPTER 7

▼

EXPECTATIONS

Matilda was feeling better these days. The morning nausea had been replaced with enhanced energy and well being. At this point, Harriet's assistance in the store wasn't necessary, but the younger woman's presence and friendship was something to which she had grown accustomed. Matilda felt that she would be rather selfish if she asked her to stay on in the store at this point, because the young mother's life was an extremely busy one. Of course, Harriet's help would be needed again during the last month of Matilda's pregnancy and until she felt able to return to assist Albert in the store after childbirth, so she would have this time to enjoy the companionship of a friend who had become very dear to her. Matilda was pondering the situation just as Harriet came in for the day.

As usual the two women had a little visit before Harriet relieved Albert at the store. "Matilda," Harriet began, "Your father still lives in Bangor doesn't her? Has he been to visit you since you learned that you were going to have a child?"

"No," replied Matilda, "And he's not likely to."

"Why on earth not? Is he in poor health and unable to travel? Bangor is only 35 miles away."

"His health isn't the concern. My father has had nothing to do with me since I married Albert instead of an extremely wealthy man he tried to convince me to wed."

"Did you love this man?"

"I couldn't stand him. He was cold and mean tempered."

"Why would your father wish to have you marry someone like that?" said Harriet, finding it difficult to believe that any father would attempt to force his daughter into a loveless marriage. "Certainly it couldn't have been for this man's wealth. From what you have told me, your father has plenty of money of his own."

"He just didn't understand. He thought I would be well provided for, live in a mansion with lots of servants and that should give me enough happiness in itself."

"My father and I were never close."

"But why? He was the only parent you had after your mother died. I should think that it would have made you especially dear to him."

"At first he seemed to blame me because my mother died having me, and also, I wasn't the son he wanted to carry on his business."

"But you couldn't help what happened to your mother. You didn't choose to be born, nor did you have a choice of whether you were a boy or a girl. How ludicrous for him to blame you!," replied Harriet, reaching over to give Matilda a hug. "Go visit your father and tell him your happy news about the baby. Surely he must miss you and will want to know about his coming grandchild."

"I can't!"

"Than I will!"

"Harriet, he disowned me!"

"What! How could he do such a thing to his child! Now I shall surely go! He must come to you and apologize. Even though he doesn't deserve it after treating you so unfairly, you both need each other."

"It will be a waste of your time, Harriet."

"We shall see," answered Harriet, her face still flushed with indignation.

Matilda smiled, while picturing this petite woman standing up to her six foot two, stern faced father. Yet if anyone could do it, Harriet can, she mused. She was one of the most gentle persons Matilda had ever known, but was capable of standing her ground against someone whom she believed had wronged another. If anyone could break through Papa's cold wall of reserve Harriet would be the most likely person to accomplish this.

CHAPTER 8

▼

A CERTAIN MISSION

Harriet slipped on her best dress, adorning it with her lovely brooch. After she had worked in the Mosby's store for six weeks, Matilda had pressed it into her hands, insisting that it represented a portion of her wages. She had been reluctant to accept it, but when finally realizing that Matilda was determined to return her much loved piece of jewelry, she did so with much gratitude. Not wishing to delay Simeon's departure for the trip to Bangor, Harriet dressed for the journey before she had told her husband that she wished to accompany him. When waiting for him to finish his chores, she donned an apron to protect her clothing from any potential soiling while she browned some chunks of beef and peeled some vegetables for a stew, which she placed in an large iron kettle, pushing it towards the back of the stove to simmer slowly for the evening meal. Amy would be in later in the morning to assist Bethiah with cooking and caring for the children, but Harriet's stew would save both women some work in preparing supper.

When Harriet heard her husband approaching, she asked, "Simeon Darling, I would like to join you on your journey to Bangor today. I have an errand to perform after you have bought the supplies."

"Of course, My Love, you know I always want your company, but I thought that you had to relieve Matilda in the store this morning," he replied.

"No, she is feeling much better now. Her morning sickness seems to be over. I won't need to assist her again until sometime in July. She is due to have her child about the 28th of that month."

"What is this mysterious 'errand' you need to perform?

"It isn't really mysterious, but…"

"But you hoped I wouldn't ask," Simeon interjected smiling.

"It's just that you probably will think it is meddling."

"My dear, you are definitely not the meddling type, but you do have your "causes," such as when you persuaded the folks at town meeting to construct a schoolhouse instead of holding classes in the church, and convinced them that even though we didn't have the fifty families here which would be enough for the General Court to force us to provide one, you gathered enough people together to build it anyway."

"But it wasn't right to use the Lord's house for a school. It is a house of worship! And look how much the upstairs room is used for social events and town meetings. Those things are not proper in God's house."

Simeon leaned over to kiss his wife, saying, "My dearest Love, you know I was proud of you for that. It was a good cause."

Then Simeon smiled while remembering that day, when Harriet, who was hardly more than a child when he married her, and how he had felt almost as though he were robbing the cradle, persuaded those stubborn men to build a schoolhouse in a fledgling community. But this young woman, who possessed a wisdom and maturity far beyond her years, never ceased to amaze him. Harriet had accomplished what Simeon had deemed impossible at that time. Again smiling in recollection, he recalled that fall day and some of the objections she had faced.

Daniel Hall, the newly elected first selectman, had said, "Mrs. Wilson, you have already convinced us to build a church before our dwelling places were scarcely livable, and now you're asking us to build a school when we don't even have fifty families here yet. If we did, the General Court would force us to do so, but we only have thirty families in this village. Also, it is 1824 and Maine has only been a state for two years. A house of worship I can sacrifice for, but aren't we doing all right with home teaching?"

"I can understand that building a school would certainly be a hardship at this point, Mr. Hall, but it could be done a little at a time and I'm sure all of us want our children to have the best educational background to prepare them for ministers, doctors, or whatever they choose," Harriet had replied. Then she added, "It would be proper, as well, to keep the church for worship instead of having all the town functions held there."

"Mrs. Wilson, let alone getting lumber and time enough to build a schoolhouse, how can we afford to support a school teacher?" Daniel Hall had asked.

"We can all take turns in boarding the teacher and each contribute a small amount for a salary." Then already anticipating the question of text books as well, Harriet added, "I would volunteer to canvass the schools of Bangor for worn books, which I will repair myself, so that expense wouldn't be a problem."

"With three youngsters and a house to run, along with your helping Bethiah birthing babies, where will you find the time for all this?" asked Daniel.

"I shall make time for it, Mr. Hall," she had replied smiling.

"But what about when we need our children's help with harvesting and farm chores?" asked Nathan Collins.

"We can easily plan classes around those times. Schedules can be worked out so neither their assistance with home chores nor their studies will be neglected."

Then suddenly, Will Sutton, John Hampton, and Nathan Collins, raised their hands, each one offering to pledge some time in the construction of the building as well as providing a portion of the lumber needed to erect it. Matt Thompson, Eli Jones, and Fred Wilkins, also offered their services for putting up the framework and flooring, as well as equal shares of lumber, and then the others followed suit. Simeon had been amazed that his wife could convince these men to construct a school house when most of them were still so busy clearing land and making their dwelling places more comfortable. He, of course, had agreed to contribute his share as well.

By the time the first fluffy snowflakes fell in November of the same year, the two story building, with its fresh red paint, was ready for its pupils. The ground floor was large enough to store wood for the fireplace in its entryway which opened into the classroom through a hallway with two doors. The second floor provided an open room which could be utilized for town meetings and any other community gatherings. The structure was built about 200 feet from the church on a parcel of land which consisted of six acres, and was already owned by the village, so fortunately, this was one issue Harriet hadn't had to cope with in her plea to construct a school. This determined young woman had once again won the support of her neighbors for a cause close to her heart. Simeon marveled at his young wife's power of persuasion. He glanced at Harriet's face, which now had the same resolute expression it had worn during the school house debate. Yes, he mused, if anyone in the universe has a chance of convincing that stubborn man to reconcile with his daughter, my amazing young wife would be the one to do so.

Simeon smiled while leaning down to kiss her and said, "My Dearest love, what is this particular cause? Is it another one as important as building the schoolhouse was?"

"Yes, this one is also," replied Harriet, while her cheeks flushed defensively. She knew her husband would not be happy with her plans to visit Mr. Clark, Matilda's father, and had hoped that Simeon would not ask her about it. She had planned to just make an excuse and slip away for a few minutes while he bought feed for the animals.

"It concerns Matilda, doesn't it?" he asked.

"How did you know?" replied Harriet, taken by surprise.

"When you returned from the store yesterday, it was written all over your face that you were deeply concerned about something. Her father lives in Bangor doesn't he?"

Harriet sighed. As usual her facial expressions could be read as easily as a book. It had been that way ever since she was a small child. Pushing a stray hair away from her cheek, she answered, "Simeon, stop reading my mind. I can't keep anything to myself!"

Simeon laughed and took her in his arms, melting away every vestige of her mild impatience with him, saying "When anyone loves his wife as much as I love mine, he literally knows her thoughts. Is that so awful, My Dearest?"

"Of course not, Harriet murmured, returning his kiss and confessing her plot to convince Mr. Clark to reunite with his pregnant daughter. By now she realized only too well that she could only resist her husband's charm momentarily. She loved him even more now than the day she met and adored him at first sight. Simeon had attached a canvas awning over the wagon which she was suddenly very grateful for, because the early June air was unseasonably warm, and soon the sun would provide as much heat as as if were August. When they approached the city, he said, "I agree that Mr. Clark has treated Matilda unfairly and cruelly, but let me speak with him, man to man." "No Simeon, I think it best that I do this. But please drive me to his place of business and wait outside for me."

Simeon was well aware of Harriet's power of persuasion, but under no circumstances would he leave her alone with a man who appeared to be so heartless, so he responded, "How about allowing me to come in from this hot sun to wait in the hallway?"

"Of course, Dearest." "How thoughtless of me."

After obtaining directions from a clerk at the town hall, Harriet took a deep breath and climbed resolutely up the marble steps to the pillared entrance of the building where Mr. Clark conducted his lumbering business. She tapped firmly on the wide oak door which had his name on a gilt edged plate.

"I'm busy. Go away, answered a man with a gruff voice.

"Please, Mr. Clark, I have come 35 miles and I have important news concerning your daughter."

"I no longer have a daughter. Go away!"

This was too much even for the gentle Harriet, when remembering the anguish in Matilda's face, while she discussed her father's harsh dealings with her. She turned the knob of unlocked door and marched in, her dark eyes flashing with anger, and faced a stern looking man in his late fifties.

"How dare you burst into my office this way! Leave at once. That is, after you apologize for your rude behavior!" he thundered.

"I am sorry that I was so discourteous, Sir, but I shall not leave until you hear me out!"

Amos Clark stared incredulously at his petite intruder. Beautiful little woman she was with red gold hair, the color of autumn leaves, and eyes like brown velvet. He was not used to anyone standing up to him, let alone a member of the female sex. Grudgingly, he said, "All right, I'll give you ten minutes." Suddenly he was amazed when he found himself attempting to hide a small smile tugging at his tight lips. No one had made him come so close to humor since his Ellen died. She was always making him laugh. He had been a different man then.

Harriet noticed the harshness in his eyes dissolve momentarily into wistfulness, mirroring the same expression his daughter had, while discussing their estrangement. Harriet said gently, "Matilda is with child. Even though she won't admit it, she longs for your love and wants you to enjoy your grandchild, who is due to be born the last week in July."

Suddenly Amos Clark's stern face was transformed with anxiety, and tears flowed down his cheeks, while he put his face down on his desk and sobbed like a child. Alarmed, Harriet rushed over and patted his back gently. "Whatever is the matter, Mr. Clark?" "News of the coming birth of a grandchild should be a happy event."

"My Mattie," he cried, "She will die like her mother! And I have been so beastly to her," he mumbled.

"Of course, she won't die. She is as healthy as can be. It was very sad about your dear wife, but most women don't die in childbirth. I have already borne three children, and I am just fine."

"A little thing like you?" he murmured.

"Yes, and many other women as well."

"How did you get here, young lady?"

"With my husband, Simeon. We came by wagon."

Would you have room in your wagon to take a stubborn old man along with you for a reunion with his daughter?"

Harriet couldn't resist giving him a hug, as she replied, "Of course, Mr. Clark"

"Better yet, come to my house for dinner tonight and spend the night. Then we shall start out early tomorrow morning," he replied, his face devoid of all its former sternness.

"What a tempting invitation," Harriet answered, "But unfortunately our folks at home would be beside themselves with worry if we don't return this evening. We have no way to contact them. Thank you for your generous offer, though, and perhaps we could stay another time."

"Of course, my dear. Whenever you are in town. I have had only myself to look after for so long, it didn't occur to me that you would have people at home who would worry. Also, in my excitement about seeing Mattie again, all I could think about was out reunion. Instead of riding in the wagon, would you accompany me in my chaise? It wouldn't take much time for me to have it brought round. It is deeply cushioned and very comfortable, and we can follow behind your husband's wagon while I learn the way to her home."

Simeon not only agreed to wait for the chaise to arrive, but also insisted that Harriet accept Mr. Clark's offer to ride with him in his comfortable buggy with its luxurious leather seats and canvas top. Also, after a brief reluctance, he agreed to allow Mr. Clark to treat the couple to a sumptuous meal, which consisted of roast beef with gravy, mashed potatoes, sweet spring peas, and strawberry short cake. I'm so grateful that Simeon and I wore our Sunday best to town, Harriet mused. Of course she had wished to look presentable when meeting with Matilda's father and also, she and Simeon had planned to dine in a small, inexpensive inn on the outskirts of town. Eating anywhere but in their own or a neighbors home was usually what the couple were accustomed to, so Mr. Clark's generosity in providing them with a delicious meal in a fancy restaurant was a special treat for them.

He had to hold his beautiful bay back a bit, to follow behind Simeon's slower horse, which was pulling a wagon full of supplies. As they rode along the winding gravel road toward home, Mr. Clark said, "Beautiful country, though remote. This area and beyond provides my lumber for shipping abroad. It is so peaceful and tranquil after the rigors of trade," he added.

Then he sat quietly, musing to himself, and later when Harriet glanced toward the handsomely attired gentleman beside her, she noticed tears sliding down his cheeks. At first she hesitated to intrude into his apparently very sad thoughts, but her sympathetic nature prevented this, so after a few moments, she asked, "What is troubling you, Mr. Clark?"

"My dear, I have been wondering how I could have treated my daughter in such a shameful way and why I became so obsessed with getting rich. I was never like that before my Ellen died."

Harriet asked, "Did you ever open your heart as you have done today?"

"No, I kept it locked up as tightly as my office safe."

"Perhaps," answered Harriet, after a long moment, "That is how you dealt with your grief."

"I believe your are correct, my wise young friend, but what a monstrous way to deal with it," he replied, while tears again rained down his cheeks.

Harriet reached over taking his large, monogrammed handkerchief from his vest pocket and dried his tears just as she would those of her children, saying, "But all that is behind you now, Mr. Clark. Just enjoy Matilda, her loving husband, and your coming grandchild now. Tell her how much you love her and she will forgive you."

"Oh I will, I will," he mumbled, managing a little smile, and leaning over to kiss Harriet's cheek, he murmured, "I feel as if I have two daughters now."

"I'm flattered, Mr. Clark, and I could use a little fatherly love. My father died when I was fourteen and my mother is still in New Brunswick."

"Happy to oblige, my dear," he replied, squeezing her hand.

Finally they came to Albert and Matilda's two-story frame home, located next to their store, and Mr. Clark, nervous about his reception, asked the couple to accompany him to the door. He needn't have worried, though, because immediately upon seeing her father, an astounded Matilda dashed outside and threw her arms around him, exclaiming, "Papa! Papa! You came! You do love me." "How did you find me?"

But before he could answer, she saw Harriet and Simeon who had stepped back just as her father entered the door, and realized that somehow her dear friend Harriet had managed to bring about this reconciliation

Amos' face was streaked with happy tears, as was his daughter's, when he responded, "My precious child, I love you more than words can express. How forgiving you are, of a stubborn, selfish man. I don't deserve such a welcome!"

"Of course you do, Papa! You came and that is all that counts." After Matilda had hugged both Harriet and Simeon, whispering her heartfelt thanks, they slipped away quietly, leaving father and daughter to their poignant reunion.

CHAPTER 9

▼

ANXIOUS FATHER

It was two o'clock in the morning, and Simeon was awakened when he heard an urgent tapping of the iron knocker against the front door. He quickly donned his robe, hurried downstairs, and when he brushed the door's curtain aside, saw Albert Mosby standing there, his face etched with anxiety. Before he had an opportunity to inform Simeon about the nature of his errand, Harriet, who had also been awakened when hearing the sound of the men's voices hurried down the stairs, because she was aware that the Mosby's child would be born any day now. Standing beside Simeon she asked, "Is Matilda having her baby now, Albert?"

"Oh yes, I think so! She's hurting really bad. I can't stand to see her suffering! Come and help her, please!" replied Albert, his hands shaking and eyes wild with concern.

"Don't worry, Albert. She will be fine. Her pregnancy has been progressing normally and there shouldn't be any problems. There is always some pain, and it will be over soon," said Harriet, patting his shaking shoulders comfortingly.

Hastily, she snatched her bag containing herbs, a sharp pair of scissors to cut the umbilical cord, as well as other midwife's necessities, flung on her clothes and climbed into Albert's chaise, which had been a surprise gift from Amos, to make the short journey to the Mosby's house. Even though the distance consisted of only one half mile, the anxious father-to-be had chosen to use the horse drawn transportation, which covered the distance more quickly that he could have running at top speed. Also, he could transport Harriet to attend to his wife more speedily by utilizing the chaise.

When they arrived, Matilda was moaning softly, and was in the mid stages of labor. Despite her discomfort, she smiled when Harriet entered the room, saying, "Now I can relax, my good friend."

"Of course you can, dear Matilda. Soon I will be placing your baby in your arms and there will be no more pain." Gently, she examined the woman who had become like a sister to her, determining that everything appeared to be progressing well, and that the baby's heartbeat was strong. She sent Albert to bring a basin with cool water and a clean white towel, which she dipped into the water, and sponged Matilda's perspiring body with it. Then she held a soothing cup of chamomile tea to her lips, which would assist in both relaxing her and easing the pain.

After a relatively short labor, especially for the birth of a first child, Harriet delivered a sturdy, nine pound son, who announced his arrival with hearty cries. Matilda's face illuminated with the joy of an ecstatic new mother, whose happiness was even more intensified, because she had waited so many years for this happy moment. She had not only borne her child with no complications, but with less pain, than most other women experienced when bearing their first babies.

Harriet, after bathing the child and his mother, and bringing Matilda some tea and a piece of toast, as well as heating some soup for Albert, left the happy couple to enjoy their long awaited parenthood. She would return each day to assist the new mother for whatever time she was needed. "Albert will take you home, Harriet," said Matilda.

"Also, he can drive by Papa's on the way home and tell him the good news."

"It is only a short walk and the crisp morning air will be invigorating. I couldn't bear to have Albert leave you and his newborn son alone, even for a few minutes. Just look at the expression on his face." Then she added, "I will stop by to tell Papa Amos about your safe delivery and his handsome grandson. I had planned to do that anyway, and he will insist on providing me with a ride from his house on the way to yours."

Matilda smiled when she saw Albert's face emanating such love and tenderness, as he gazed at her and his son, and the happiness on their ecstatic faces, would be forever etched in Harriet's psyche. Not only was Albert relieved that his wife's childbirth pain was over, but the couple had almost lost hope that they would ever become parents.

"Then Matilda said, "Harriet, my dear friend, please change your mind and accept the offer of a ride. You must be exhausted! The baby and I will be just fine. It will only take a few minutes. After that he can go to tell Papa the good news."

"Matilda, you need to get some rest now," and then with an impish smile, she added, "You know how stubborn I am, and under no circumstances, will I leave you alone."

Quickly Harriet left the happy family and hurried to inform the expectant grandfather of the birth of his grandson.

Amos had built his house just a quarter of a mile from the home of his daughter and son in law almost immediately after their reconciliation, as well as selling both his house and lumber business in Bangor. After all their years apart, he wished to be as near to his daughter as possible. Also, despite Harriet's continuing assurance that Matilda would not lose her life during childbirth as her mother had, he was deeply concerned. Harriet smiled while she walked rapidly to his home. She could hardly wait to tell this man, whom she had learned to love as a surrogate father, of the happy event. He will be so relieved that Matilda came through childbirth safely and won't he be delighted to have a grandchild! She mused. While tapping gently on his door, her thoughts wandered momentarily to the first time she had done so under such extremely different circumstances. No one would ever believe that this loving, giving man Amos had become, had been the gruff, alienated person he had been just a few months before. It had not occurred to her that it was not the usual calling hours, although she did know that he was an early riser. When he promptly answered her knock, his face was ashen. He blurted, "My Mattie! Is she…? What has happened?"

Harriet, in her excitement concerning the happy news, had thought nothing of the reaction Amos might have of such an early morning visit because of his concern for daughter's survival during childbirth, and of course he knew that she was likely to have her baby any day now.

"Oh, Papa Amos! Mattie is just fine and has given birth to a very healthy, nine pound boy. I am so sorry I alarmed you. I just wished to give you the joyful news as soon as possible."

"Oh, My Dear! What wonderful news! I am so grateful for your coming!" Then he embraced the young woman whom he loved not only as a daughter, but as the person responsible for his having more happiness and fulfillment after his reconciliation with his daughter than he had ever dreamed possible. Then he said, "My Child, let me take you home and give me that heavy bag you are carrying at once. You must have been up all night. Then I shall go to see my Mattie and my grandson."

Suddenly tears of joy rained down his face and she took his handkerchief from his pocket and wiped them away just as she had done that day while they rode towards his daughter's home for their reunion.

CHAPTER 10

▼

CHORES AND REWARDS

From the parlor window, Harriet marveled at the fragile green draperies hanging from ancient maples, which stood about twenty feet from the left side of the house, and a verdant carpet of grass so lush that it seemed improbable just three weeks ago, an April blizzard had covered everything with a cold, white blanket. The long, frigid winter had been reluctant to release its icy grip and this balmy day filled Harriet's heart with hopeful expectancy. Simeon's return should be any day now, she mused. Perhaps it would be in time for the birth of the new life which blossomed within her. Momentarily, worry lines etched her forehead, while wondering if Bethiah's strength would be sufficient for delivering the baby. The strong movements of the child reassured her that all was well with her pregnancy, despite her grueling winter, which had demanded so much from her, both physically and emotionally. At least it should be a birth without complications and that would be less taxing for Bethiah. She whispered a quick prayer of thanks, and impulsively slipped outside and knelt a moment to touch the soft carpet of grass lovingly. How she longed to walk barefooted through the sweet scented greenery with the spring sun caressing her face and its gentle breezes tousling her hair. Although sensing Harriet's yearnings, Bethiah went to the window and observed her beloved daughter-in-law carefully raise her body, heavy with child, and walk towards the barn to feed the animals. So young, and so much demanded of her, she mused. She was amazed with Harriet's endurance and strength, because she was small boned and had a fragile appearance. Bethiah often wondered how she managed all the heavy work throughout the longest, coldest winter she ever remembered having experienced.

Joshua hadn't been able to assist in the daily chores because he had become so frail, and it was heartrending for Bethiah while she observed the pain mirrored so poignantly in his eyes, when he watched his son's wife "in the family way" as he put it, struggle with heavy pieces of wood, let alone having to chop it up after the supply of stove ready wood which Simeon, who hadn't planned for the unusually cold winter, had left, not realizing that it would be depleted before his return in April. Also, he hadn't planned to work in the distant forests during the winter as he had done the previous year, but once again, their crops had been disappointing and cash was so badly needed, he had no alternative. How Simeon had dreaded leaving his family, especially with his father feeling so poorly. Harriet hadn't told him about her pregnancy, because she didn't wish to have him worrying about her as well. Joshua had been upset when his daughter-in-law performed the barn work, and also, on those occasions, which were becoming quite frequent, when he would he return from the woodshed, white with fatigue, and Harriet would finally persuade the gallant old man, after much reluctance on his part, to allow her to attend the duties which he felt that he should be performing. Bethiah's eyes clouded with tears while wondering how much longer she would have him. Where had the 47 years gone since the day that they, so exuberant with youth, had stood in front of that young minister, pledging their vows? While she envisioned the tall, handsome young man he had been, her eyes filled with tears, which she hurriedly wiped away with her apron, because she didn't wish to have anyone see her crying. Then her face suddenly became illuminated with a beauty which belied her years. For a few brief moments they were in Taunton, both young again, dancing to Grandpa Allen's fiddle music while they celebrated their wedding.

Harriet was milking Bessie when she felt the familiar surge of liquid. Not wishing to leave the animal half milked and uncomfortable, she finished the chore, carefully exited from the milking stool, and headed for the house. Bethiah was waiting for her at the door. The experienced midwife had observed all the "signs" early that morning. Within only an hour, she placed Harriet's fourth child, a sturdy, heartily vocal, boy into her waiting arms.

Outside, a light rain gently tapped the roof and after a short nap which was firmly insisted upon by Bethiah, Harriet awakened to its calm sound which had always made her feel cozy and peaceful. After checking her small son, whose dark fluff of hair promised to be similar to the thick wavy hair of his father, Harriet went to the window to gaze outside as she had done after the birth of her other children. She basked in an ecstasy almost beyond description, just as she had experienced after the birth of Simeon Jr., Jenny, and Elizabeth. God seemed so close and it appeared as though everything she viewed was even more beautiful than it had been previously...the grass more verdant, the rain droplets on the new leaves more jewel like, and the mauve, pink, soft green, and pale gold of the emerging rainbow in the clearing sky, even lovelier than all the others she had seen. Harriet felt one with the universe. She was standing there, with the splendor of nature flooding her soul when Simeon's tall, lean form appeared in the door. While he folded her within his embrace, he was amazed anew with his wife's radiant beauty. He stood there holding her until his newborn son announced his presence with a hearty cry, and then gazed lovingly at the baby's face, who Bethiah had remarked, was a mirror image of his when he had been born. His name, James, had been previously selected, because after Elizabeth had been born, the couple decided to name the next son after Harriet's grandfather. Simeon held little Jamie in his arms until the infant fell asleep, and then after kissing the baby's soft little cheek placed him carefully in the cradle which Joshua had built. While gazing lovingly at his tiny son, he wondered why Harriet hadn't told him she was with child before he left for the deep woods. Had he known, leaving her with so much responsibility and heavy work would have been unthinkable. And of course, he reasoned, that is why she deliberately opted not to do so. Harriet knew that I would have remained at home had she told me that she was expecting a child. Simeon never ceased to be amazed at the courage and devotion of his remarkable young wife.

CHAPTER 11

▼

A NEW WAY OF LIFE

After Bethiah's urging and offer to watch the children, Harriet headed for the small wild flower dappled patch of meadow behind the barn and stretched out on its verdant carpet. Her mountains of laundry finished, this peaceful place with its cushiony grass, provided a special haven for rest. Simeon, having seen her lying there one day, left it unmowed for her to enjoy. The sun-warmed earth released vigor to rejuvenate Harriet's tired body, and she gazed at the sky, blue as a lake, with its cotton fluff clouds, until its bright intensity caused her to shield her eyes. Basking in serenity, she closed her eyes, feeling one with the earth, the trees, and the sky until she dozed off, lulled into peaceful slumber.

Less than an hour later, she was suddenly jostled awake by a thunderclap, followed by the sound of pounding hooves. Jumping up, she looked in horror towards the upper hayfield, where Simeon was being dragged by a terrified horse, with one of his legs tangled in the reins. When the mare, frightened by an unusually loud crash of thunder, observed Harriet racing towards her, she slowed her pace and then stopped. She had always had a calming effect on animals.

"Simeon, my dearest!" gasped Harriet, while kneeling down beside her husband's inert form, listening for a heartbeat. Her lips moving in prayer, she finally heard its weak, but comforting sound, quiet as a whisper. With a strength beyond her own, she lifted him upon the horse's back, climbed up beside him, and managed to transport him home.

Gold Fox, saddened by the migration of his Indian guardians, rode slowly, wondering where he should go in his quest to find someplace to make his home among his white brothers. The Indians had moved deeper into Canada, because their hunting grounds and source of furs had been depleted by the settlers. He had attempted to join them, because they were the only family he had known for ten years, but Chief Long Horn had dissuaded him saying, "My Son, you must leave us and teach your white brothers how to cherish the earth and its animals or nothing will remain. A few of them are wise and take just what they need from the earth, but many others are wasteful and ravage her."

Reluctantly Gold Fox agreed. I suppose I must think of myself as Jonathan when beginning my new life as a white man, he mused sadly. After experiencing a strange sense of urgency, he decided to visit the area where the young family in the ox cart had traveled to make their home. He often wondered how they were managing in that place not much larger than many of the Indian camping grounds. After reaching his destination, and descending a steep hill, he gazed down towards a field, and saw the young woman with the red-gold hair, with a small boy alongside her, struggling to fill a hay wagon. Clouds, dark and menacing hovered overhead, while the gaps between each thunderclap grew closer together.

Within an instant, he was beside her, scooping large forkfuls of hay into the wagon before the approaching storm ruined the sun-dried hay. If it were harvested when wet, it would mildew in the lofts and be unfit for the animals' consumption. Without taking even a moment to introduce himself, Jonathan joined the mother and son in their frantic efforts to pitch the remainder of the hay into the large body of the wagon before the downpour began. All three worked tirelessly, and just as the first silver needles of rain fell against their perspiring faces, the now calmed horse hauled it into the shelter of the barn, filled with its precious cargo—the season's last load of the winter's hay supply to nourish the livestock.

"I can't begin to express my gratitude," Harriet said, pushing a strand of wet hair from her forehead. Without your help, most of that hay would have remained in the field, getting ruined in this downpour. My husband just suffered a concussion and a broken leg. He was dragged by his horse and must have struck his head on a rock. My father-in-law is unwell and all the neighbors are busy with their own haying. Bethiah, my mother-in-law, is nursing my husband, so until you came, there was just Simeon Jr. and I to complete this task.

"I'm so thankful you came by." She added, sensing a strange familiarity while studying the young man's features. There is something about him, she mused. I feel as though I have seen him before. Oh dear, it must be my imagination, she reasoned. Jonathan remained with the family to assist them until Simeon's leg had healed and he was strong enough to resume his many farm duties. The lonely young man had enjoyed having been within the atmosphere of a loving family who regarded him as though he were part of it. His visit with them also assisted him in adapting to his new life away from his Indian friends, who had been such a vital part of his life for so many years. During his sojourn with these warm-hearted people, he had slept in the loft with the children, and loved listening to their happy chatter as they drifted off to sleep each night. But with four children, their grandparents, as well as Harriet and Simeon, Jonathan was aware that the modest little home was crowded and thought it best to move on even though the family urged him to remain with them.

Simeon had told him that if he insisted upon leaving, the best place to find work would probably be in Bangor, because of its paper mill and other various places of business. Jonathan found a job in the mill and worked there for a while, but its atmosphere was so alien to his outdoor living, that he longed for the open spaces and decided to move on, seeking work on a farm or perhaps even in the building trade. At the mill, he found that he learned the skills needed for his work there quickly, so perhaps could learn carpentry as well, which would provide him with the opportunity to be outside the confines of a building at least during a portion of his working hours, so he gave his notice, and went on his way to pursue another way of making a living.

CHAPTER 12

▼

FUTILE ATTEMPTS

Jonathan, weary from searching for work in the surrounding townships, headed his faithful pony towards the deep forest. With spring coming, he had been told that there would be logging drives. Since this work required the skill and agility in which his years with his Indian brothers, whose daily tasks required much of the same physical abilities, his experience would be beneficial in this type of occupation. Quite possibly the logging operations could use another hand. His reluctance in making a decision to earn money for his living in this type of employment wasn't the danger of log driving. The factor deterring him was the distaste he harbored for mass lumbering, which decimated the woodlands. Unfortunately, every household he had approached asking for work had the same plight—an extremely harsh winter which had drained their meager stores for their own families, and that taking on a hired man to feed, even if he asked for only room and board in lieu of wages, was not a feasible prospect. Because of these circumstances, Jonathan felt that he had no other alternative but to seek employment in the logging trade.

Jonathan was always hungry these days and he foraged in the woods for acorns he could grind into meal and caches of corn the Indians had left behind when leaving for Canada. He caught a few fish now and then, by cutting a hole in the ice and dipping his handmade line into the frigid water. Jonathan couldn't bear to hunt animals for meat. Every time his hunger would tempt him to do so, he thought about how difficult it was for them to subsist themselves, as well as escaping from their natural predators, and these feelings deterred him from killing animals for his sustenance. Even as a small child, he hated to eat meat. In his hazy childhood memories before his being orphaned by the war and his rescue by the Indians, he remembered his mother being frustrated by this, not understanding his feelings. Most people didn't, because the settlers were so dependent on game for their meat supply. Jonathan even disliked having to eat fish. They also were living, breathing things. Whenever one of the farm animals had been slaughtered for meat, Jonathan ran beyond the meadow behind the barn to hide in a sheltering group of pines which formed a little circle of tranquility, whose distance was great enough from the butchering area for him to escape its horrific accompanying sounds. Upon reflection of these memories, he wondered why he could remember those concerning his aversion to killing animals for meat and had no recollection of what had happened to his parents nor the events which had taken place just before the Indians had rescued him after finding him alone and terrified. Just attempting to remember filled him with sensations of deep sadness, so as always he avoided further contemplation on the matter.

After traveling for about five miles, Jonathan stopped to rest his pony and was tremendously relieved to discover a small spring beside the narrow path he had been following. He watered his thirsty animal, and then dropped down on the ground, lying on his stomach, and savored long draughts from its refreshing coolness. While filling his canteen with water for both himself and his pony, he looked at his reflection mirrored in the water's dark surface, and scarcely recognized himself. He looked like some half-starved man who hadn't eaten a decent meal for months, which was an accurate portrayal of his present condition. Despite his reluctance to work amongst these fallen trees, he had few if any other options. At least he would try to convince the person in charge of the logging operation to change his method of lumbering if he were the one responsible for slaughtering this area of the forest. While remounting his pony to continue his quest, he said, "Old girl, perhaps it won't be so bad. Maybe the boss of this group of loggers may have had the wisdom to plan the cutting areas wisely, leaving sufficient space between the trees in order to leave a portion of the them standing, instead of felling each one in his path."

His pony lifted her head, whinnying as if to answer, then shaking it as if in disagreement. "Unfortunately, you are probably right, my faithful friend," Jonathan murmured sadly. For the greater portion of his life, the woodlands had provided a home for him that was much more desirable than any mansion which could be built. The skittering sounds of animals scampering through the brush, the fragrance of evergreens, and the chic, chic, chickadee of that tiny, stalwart bird, filled Jonathan with such a sensation of peace, that it seemed as though he were Gold Fox again, in his forest home with his Indian brothers, sitting around the campfire. Jonathan dismounted to enjoy this brief interval as well as to give his pony a few minutes to rest. While he leaned against an ancient oak, he watched the golden glints of the noon sun, sparkling the crevices in some rocks with miniature diamonds, and gilding the edges of leaves with golden flecks. For that transcendent moment, the gnawing in his stomach subsided, as if this tranquil beauty sustained his hunger, providing him with another type of satiety.

By mid afternoon, Jonathan had traveled to an area of the forest where the ring of axes shattered its aura of peacefulness, and whose invasive echoes hushed the birdsong, sending all four footed creatures scurrying for cover. Then he saw it. The devastation was much worse than he could have imaged. Countless stumps of trees for miles—a ruthless sweep through the woodlands which had felled every tree without leaving even a sapling. What had been a virgin forest with lofty trees, whose fingers brushed the sky and soughed in summer breezes, was now a barren wasteland. Anger consumed him and stimulated his adrenalin to the point where he no longer felt hunger nor weariness. In a manner quite unlike his usually calm and gentle nature, he made no attempt to contain his rage, when he confronted a tall, large-framed man, who appeared to be in charge of the crew continuing the pillaging in an adjoining stretch of the woods.

"Sir, why has every tree been felled in such a large section, leaving none of the smaller ones to mature?" asked Jonathan, who at this point was trying to keep his anger under control.

Rufus Ingham wiped the sweat off his face with an impatient swipe of his red bandana, and while glaring at the shabby, emaciated stranger, retorted, "What business is it of yours and what are you doing here anyway?"

"I am looking for work, but now I don't want any part of this wholesale plundering of the forest. I just want to attempt to convince you to spare some of the trees as you proceed in your lumbering," Jonathan replied.

"Don't preach to me and tell me how to do my work unless you want trouble and plenty of it! Besides, there's lots more trees," Rufus answered, glowering menacingly. He was exhausted and there was two hours of daylight remaining for the day's work. At this point instead of listening to this meddlesome stranger all Rufus desired was to finish his day's labor, have a good hot meal at the cook shack, and relax for the evening in the bunkhouse. He had enough trouble with his own men to keep them from fighting among themselves during their long winter of confinement without this ragtag agitator bothering him. Anyway, it wasn't as though he was going to ask his crew to pile all the logs up and make a giant bonfire or leave them to rot on the ground. The wood would be used for shipbuilding, houses, and even churches, Rufus reasoned with himself after experiencing a faint pang of guilt, while observing the sea of stumps. Perhaps this is why he added to his angry reply to Jonathan in a less hostile tone, "It's easier to cut them this way. We don't have time to keep moving about picking this tree or that one. It would take twice as long."

"But it's wrong! It will take years to replenish those you have already felled and since you have also cut the saplings there will be great stretches of barren land which upsets the balance of nature. Floods will come and much wildlife will be displaced."

"Stop interfering with our work and get out of our way," yelled Rufus, his face again flushed with anger. "We don't need philosophers around here either. We need hard working men."

Disregarding the angry man's command, Jonathan jumped in front of the next tree they attempted to cut, clinging to it with all the strength he possessed, replying, "I will stay right here until you agree to spare some of the trees as you continue your cutting."

Enraged, Rufus lunged at Jonathan, wrenching him away from the tree with a swift thrust of his powerful arms. Had Jonathan not been weakened by lack of food, it wouldn't have been so easy to dislodge him. Also, he wouldn't have lost his balance which caused him to plummet against a large stump protruding from the ground and strike his head against a rock when falling.

Jonathan was still unconscious when Simeon, who had again been forced to spend another winter in the woods, because of a second year of a scanty harvest, arrived from the area of his cutting which was in a more dense portion of the forest. When he heard the angry voice of his boss, he knew there was trouble and broke into a dead run. Simeon usually served as a peacemaker among the men when they started bickering and this time it appeared as if there were a real problem. As he reached the area of the disturbance, he was horrified to see a pale, gaunt young man lying on the ground, motionless. Quickly he dropped down on his knees and listened for a heartbeat in the chest of the inert man. So greatly altered was Jonathan's appearance after his months of hardship, it took a few moments to recognize him. Simeon was shocked when realizing that this hollow cheeked fellow was Jonathan, the kind young person who had assisted Harriet when he had been injured, in getting the hay safely harvested and into the barn before the drenching rain of the swiftly approaching thunderstorm ruined it. Afterwards, Jonathan had set his leg which had been broken when it became entangled with his horse's reins while he had been dragged through the field.

Then Simeon exclaimed, "Jonathan, Jonathan! Dear Friend! Please speak to me." While leaning his face closer to the injured man's chest, he heard nothing except a tiny fluttering sound. "Lord, Oh Lord, please let him be all right," he prayed.

Simeon dashed into the cook's shack, found a cold, wet cloth, and placed it upon Jonathan's forehead. Next, he attempted artificial respiration such he as would have done for a drowning person, but the minute response within the quiet form was too feeble to show any movement. Meanwhile, Jonathan's pony was nuzzling her fallen master's face with her tongue.

"How did this happen," demanded Simeon. "Who did this to him?"

"I did," replied Rufus, "But I didn't intend to hurt him this way. He was interfering with our work, holding on to that tree and claiming he would stay there until we stopped cutting all the trees in our path. He wanted us to sashay around picking and choosing to leave some of them standing, 'So it wouldn't upset the balance of nature.' "High falluting talk and not practical at all. Besides, who gave him the right to come barging in disrupting our work? Anyway, when I pulled him away from the tree he was holding on to, trying to keep us from cutting trees like we'd been doing, he went flying right into that stump and bounced off and hit his head against it."

"So he had the courage to voice what I've been feeling all along and was too concerned with my need for money to articulate. Help me make a litter so his pony can haul it into the village where I can get him some medical help. He can't stay on his horse, even if we put him on it."

"Put him on a bunk and perhaps he'll come to later," replied Rufus.

"What if he doesn't?" "A man's life may be at stake!"

"Well, you're not leaving! The drive is next week and I need all the able bodied men I have!" Rufus bellowed.

"I must! He needs help now!"

"If you go, you're fired. You might not return in time for the drive."

"Then fire me," snapped Simeon angrily. "I'm leaving."

"Then go! I don't need two troublemakers around here. The Paymaster will bring your wages around to that general store in your village after the drive is over. Now get on with you!"

While Simeon was constructing the litter, Ben, his neighbor, who's financial hardships had also forced him into lumbering, came in from his work in the woods, helped Simeon finish it, and got a blanket from the bunkhouse to cushion Jonathan's yet unconscious form while his pony hauled him through the miles of woods to the village.

When Rufus sank into his bunk, cushioned with fresh evergreens, he didn't drift off to sleep in his usual manner which was almost immediate slumber the minute he sank down into the balsam cushion that formed his mattress. As weary as he was from his long, backbreaking labor of the day, he couldn't relax. All he could think of was what if that meddlesome stranger didn't wake up? He didn't intend to hurt him that badly, and he was sorry for that, but he reasoned, if he hadn't been making trouble it wouldn't have happened. Also, even more worrisome to Rufus was whether he would be held responsible by law if the man didn't recover? Finally after tossing and turning for what seemed like most of the night, he finally drifted off into an uneasy slumber.

The sun had just climbed the hills, displaying its golden hues when a fatigued Simeon, who had refused to ride the weary pony hauling her unconscious master on the fifteen mile trek through the forest reached his destination and the expert hands of his mother. Her medical skills, gleaned trough her years of ministering to the sick, wounded or victims to the many accidents, which faced her family and neighbors, in addition to the numerous childbirths in which she served as a midwife, rivaled those of a skilled physician. Simeon's tired eyes illuminated in a smile, thinking with pride of his gentle, courageous mother, who had helped save so many lives in their remote little township, 35 miles away from the nearest doctor, and his dear Harriet, who was so young, but yet so brave and capable. Having been tutored by his mother, she was quickly absorbing the same vital skills. When he finally arrived at the family homestead, they both ran out to meet him, and after brief hugs and kisses of welcome, quickly attended to their injured friend. Bethiah examined Jonathan's head for injuries, gently encircling it with her competent hands. She felt a large swollen lump on his head, but found that his skull didn't appear to be fractured. After cleansing the wound, Bethiah poured fresh water into a bowl, added a some arnica tincture, soaked a linen cloth in the solution, and wrapped it around Jonathan's forehead, easing it gently over the large lump protruding from the back of his head. Then with her kindly eyes filled with concern said while loosening Jonathan's tattered buckskin shirt to assist in his breathing, "The arnica should ease the pain and help heal whatever bruise might appear. Also, I believe that his remaining in a stupor is prolonged because of lack of proper nourishment and fatigue which is probably the reason he hasn't regained consciousness at this point."

The two women, accustomed to working together when nursing the injured or delivering babies, made Jonathan comfortable quickly, despite their initial shock when observing their friend in such a deplorable condition. After they gently removed his boots, which had little of their soles remaining, and covered him with a warm blanket to assist him in resting more comfortably, Harriet hurried into the kitchen to heat some broth for the emaciated young man as soon as became conscious.

Within minutes, Jonathan moaned a few times, and his eyes fluttered open. Looking around at the familiar faces etched with concern, he managed a weak smile. "Thank God," murmured Simeon, who had refused food or drink himself, until his friend responded to Bethiah's nursing.

After drinking the cup of tea Bethiah held to his lips, Jonathan felt strong enough to sip the nourishing spoonfuls of broth Harriet fed him. After finishing it, he drifted off into a peaceful sleep.

"Oh, no," Simeon said, his eyes filled with renewed concern.

"He is going to be fine," Bethiah responded. "He needs his rest now and when he awakens he will be much stronger. See how the color is already returning to his face," she added, patting Simeon's arm with a motherly touch. "Now eat your own meal and relax. You look almost as pale and weary as he does. However, I will watch to see that he does awaken before too lengthy an interval, because when one has a concussion, he must not sleep too long without moving about a little."

That evening when Harriet and Simeon finally flew into one another's arms for a belated welcome, she lay quiet and peaceful beside her beloved husband, who had almost immediately fallen into an exhausted slumber. Harriet, though ecstatic because of his return, was restless. Her thoughts soon drifted to Jonathan. Something flickered within her memory, vague but persistent, concerning an injury which occurred many years ago involving herself and her cousin when they were both around ten years of age. These recollections from the past began when she noticed the thin white scar in the center of Jonathan's right hand. She tried to remember what made it seem familiar to her. Then finally while half awake, half asleep, visions of herself, her Uncle James and her cousin, whose name was also Jonathan, flitted trough her mind. Her Uncle had taken them fishing and while they walked along the tree lined path towards home, Jonathan had broken into a run, challenging Harriet to a race. Suddenly he tripped and fell, cutting his hand on a sharp rock. After the wound healed, it left a scar very similar to the one on the hand of this older, yet hauntingly familiar, Jonathan. Also, the hair color of the young man sleeping so peacefully on the couch was the same red-gold shade as her cousin's had been ten years ago, while the War of 1812 raged, and Uncle James, Aunt Clara and Jonathan had disappeared. Of course, many boys were named Jonathan, had the same color of hair and had scars from various injuries, she reasoned. However, her memories were persistent and she decided to discuss them with him when he regained some of his vigor and then suddenly realized that all she had to do was to ask him what his surname was. That is if he remembered it. He had not mentioned it during the time he had spent with the family previously, and merely introduced himself as Jonathan. Then finally after much contemplation on the matter, she nestled contentedly in her husband's arms, caressing his cheek gently, to avoid awakening him from his exhausted slumber, and soon drifted peacefully off to sleep.

The next morning Jonathan awakened just as the pale gold shafts of sun flitted through the lace of the parlor curtains. Lifting his head from the comfortable couch where he had spent the night, he felt only a twinge of pain from his wound which had been neatly bandaged by Bethiah's expert fingers. What a wonderful caring family, these people are, he mused. They seemed even more familiar to him now than when he had experienced vague stirrings within his psyche alluding to something deeply submerged his foggy past, after observing Harriet in the ox cart, while he had followed the young family during their journey through a remote, deeply forested area to provide protection for them from whatever dangers which they might have been subjected Since the loss of his parents, he had lost much of his memory and what their fate had been yet remained a mystery. He couldn't even recall his surname. Just as Harriet tiptoed in to see if he required any additional care, horrific recollections surged through his being, and he feigned sleep until she left the room. A few moments later, he staggered to his feet, went outside and leaned against the sturdy shingles of the barn, breaking into uncontrollable sobbing—finally releasing his grief which had been buried so deeply within his subconscious. After the sudden return of his memory, he was reliving the horror, which he had experienced during the murder of his parents by the soldiers, who had also looted and burned their home. When regaining his composure, he went to the well, brought up a pail of water and doused his face with it.

After finding his bed empty, Harriet went outside to search for him, meeting him as he approached the kitchen door. "It's all right," he said. "I just had to be alone for a little while. I finally remembered who I really am. I am Jonathan Jennings, your cousin. After recalling the terrible fate of my parents, I believe that my shock and fear must have been so intense that it must have caused my loss of memory. When that lumber boss pushed me, I must have fallen and struck my head against something hard, at least according to the size of the lump on the back of my head. The impact must have revived it."

"Oh, Cousin Jonathan!" Harriet exclaimed, hugging him, "How terrible! Poor Uncle James and Aunt Clara! And what a traumatic thing for you, just a little boy! Who cared for you after that?"

"Some friendly Indians came by and took me to their campgrounds and then they raised me as one of their own sons. I don't know what would have become of me if they hadn't come along. I found later that most of our town had been burned, so I don't know who else was nearby. I never could have managed without them."

"How kind of those Indians. Where are they now?"

"They went deeper into Canada. Most of their hunting grounds and land had been taken over by the colonists and much of its resources had been depleted. They had trouble finding enough furs for their needs, and fish was becoming scarce."

"It's sad they had to leave. Many of the settlers have been very wasteful. I suppose that when they arrived in a country so bountiful as it was then, they must have thought that its resources were endless. Simeon and I have often discussed this problem," answered Harriet. Then she added, "I have felt a familiarity about you for some time and last night when I saw that little white scar on your hand, I remembered when I was a child visiting from New Brunswick, I had a cousin Jonathan who was racing with me and fell cutting his hand when Uncle James took us fishing several years ago, and wondered if you were that Jonathan. I am so happy that you have returned, safe and sound! We had almost given up hope of ever seeing you again."

Then she noticed his eyes, reddened by tears he had tried so desperately to conceal from her when he had left his bed, still weak from his head injury. How painful it must have been when he remembered what had happened to is parents, she mused. His face revealed the agony which that ten year old boy had experienced, so traumatic that his mind had refused to accept it for such a long time. Perhaps never, if it were not for that blow on the head. How strange, she pondered, that because of his injury, he had recalled his past. She would wait until he was ready to tell the other members of the family of their relationship and after he had returned to his bed to rest for a while longer, before discussing the sad boyhood tragedy he had experienced. Jonathan slept through breakfast and by dinner time was ready to have a family reunion with these warm, loving people—his own relatives, who had also been dear friends as well.

Later during the evening meal, Amy suddenly appeared. After having heard about Simeon's return, she burst into the room without knocking despite her usual shyness and natural propriety, expecting to hear that Ben was also on his way home.

"When will Ben return?" she asked. "Why didn't you all come home together?"

"He had to remain in the for forest a while longer to work on the logging drive," Simeon answered reluctantly, watching the cloud of sadness descending over the features of the disappointed young wife. "We had to leave to get medical assistance for Jonathan who had been injured."

Amy bit her lip to restrain herself from shedding the tears which welled up like a suppressed fountain threatening to overflow and ran outside. Harriet darted after the distraught young woman, taking her into her arms and comforting her until her sobs subsided. Then she invited Amy to remain to share the family's evening meal and join them in celebrating her lost cousin's return. Amy bravely apologized for her outburst, saying "I just didn't believe that Ben would stay for the log drive. He promised me that he wouldn't. He has no experience on log driving and it's so dangerous." Then she gratefully accepted the offer to have supper with the family and said, "I guess it would be good for me to stay here awhile tonight and to have a happy event to look forward to, rather leaving for home immediately and probably spending the evening feeling sad about Ben's not coming home yet. I will fetch little Ben. He and Elizabeth are still outside playing."

Simeon was surprised to find sufficient food remaining in the family larder. He had been deeply concerned, almost dreading to ask about their supply. Then Harriet told him about her working in the store for Matilda, who was finally expecting a child after eight years of marriage, during the mornings when she felt unwell. In exchange, she received food and supplies. Although Simeon was relieved that his family was provided for and proud of Harriet for her finding a way obtain it, he was disturbed because his already overworked wife had taken on yet another task. He asked, "My Dearest, with all your housework and caring for the family, as well as the extra chores you performed while I was away, how did you manage to add the store duties to your workload without tiring yourself too much?"

"Mother Wilson and Amy helped with the children and working at the store wasn't tiring. In fact I rather enjoyed it. Matilda and I became very good friends. She was happy when she learned that I could do arithmetic and felt comfortable when dealing with customers. Also, because her mother died when giving birth to her, I believe that having another woman around for a while, who had already borne several children without any problems, assisted in easing any fears Matilda might have experienced about giving birth to a baby. In fact, Matilda mentioned once that although she wanted a baby very much was a little frightened when first learning that she was with child."

"You are a resourceful wife, My Love," replied Simeon. "I am very proud of you. Also, I am glad you were there to allay some of Matilda's anxieties about her pregnancy and that you two have become good friends."

"We are almost like sisters and both enjoy so many of the same activities, such as reading books, such as those written by Susanna Rowson, the poetry of Milton and Chaucer, and also, we love the music of Brahms, Mozart, and Beethoven, as well as admiring the paintings of Benjamin West and John Singleton Copley. We both hope that sometime we can visit Boston to attend a concert or visit some book stores, but probably that will be after we are both old and gray," Harriet added, laughing.

Simeon smiled, and when giving her a hug replied, "Perhaps something can be arranged for that outing a little sooner than that."

After Joshua, with his eyes filled with that sad expression which was growing increasingly more frequent because of his feelings concerning the activities he was now physically unable to perform, told him that Harriet had to do the barn chores, chop wood, and attend to her household duties as well as working at the store, Simeon felt even more determined to do something special for his young wife, who had shouldered such a heavy workload for so long. At least I'm glad that I bought that nice stove for Harriet, Simeon mused. He found it easy to see why it was called a step stove, with its oven sitting on top and the flat cooking surface below. This useful invention featured a firebox, which opened in front of the stove to receive its wood supply. It required much less effort for Harriet than when she used the fireplace for cooking. Also, the stove offered a great deal more safety and comfort when preparing meals than she experienced while standing close to the fireplace's flames. The cook stove's oven was much safer than the one in the wall beside the fireplace. On several occasions, she had just managed to escape having been burned when reaching inside it to test its temperature. Not only did this wonderful new contrivance lighten Harriet's work load, but it assisted in the heating of the house as well. Also, the stove required much less wood than the fireplace used, and provided steadier, more concentrated heat. It had been well worth the $15.00 dollars he had paid for it even though its purchase cut deeply into his monetary resources. Although Simeon realized how much the stove meant to Harriet, after the long difficult winter and all her extra work, he felt that he must provide his dear wife with some much needed leisure activity. As soon as possible he would attempt to take her on a trip to Boston, but at the present time, he could at least take her to a dance planned for Saturday evening. The event would take place in the schoolhouse, utilizing the building's second floor and music would be provided by fiddlers as well as banjo players. Harriet loved to dance. He smiled while remembering how they had met in New Brunswick during a similar event, held on the school's second floor as well. When he escorted her to the dance in this particular structure, it was a place she had been largely responsible for having been built. While they swirled to the lively pace of the music, Harriet's face was glowing with pleasure and her appearance was as young and carefree as it had been before bearing four children and having shouldered so many responsibilities while he had been away.

CHAPTER 13

▼

DUTIES

Harriet stood at the kitchen window gazing at the sudden transformation of the trees which were now verdant with bright new foliage. Except for the faithful old oak which had clung to its tissue thin brown leaves until the first tiny buds appeared, the stark forms of the other trees had seemed devoid of life since their autumn radiance had fallen to make a transient bright carpet below. Through the open window, a breeze, scented with the essence of spring, tousled her hair and she felt the warmth of the sun in its touch. This time of the year always filled Harriet with amazement and she felt a childlike joy each spring as if it were always a wonderful new surprise. Impulsively, she ran outside and dropped on her knees to touch the fragile bloom of a violet nestled in the verdant new grass. For a few moments, Harriet reflected upon all the many useful skills she had learned from Bethiah She and her dear mother-in-law had just finished making a new supply of soap from fat saved from drippings and lye made from ashes gleaned from the fireplace. It was a time consuming task, which began with making lye by placing the ashes in the large tub Joshua had prepared for the process. He had bored a hole near its bottom to provide a tap for the liquid to flow from, and when it was ready to be drained. Harriet tied an old apron around her waist, filled the barrel with ashes, and poured boiling water over them.

"These ashes are mostly from oak firewood and they make the strongest lye, but I think that the soap made from apple tree wood is whiter," Bethiah commented.

"Oh, that's why some batches colors vary," replied Harriet. "I didn't know that the type of tree used for firewood made a difference in the making of soap."

After the lye was ready they placed the fat drippings they had saved along with lard enough to make the amount of grease required for their batch of soap. Next they added the prepared lye and placed the mixture to boil on the rack of the little outdoor fireplace Simeon had built, utilizing stones from the rock pile. When the mixture looked as if it were ready, Bethiah scooped up a small portion, cooling it to see if any grease appeared on the top.

"Yes," she sighed in relief, "This is just right. It's going to be a good batch of soap. If it were greasy on the top, we would need to pour in additional lye and boil it some more."

Harriet's eyes filled with concern as she glanced at her dear mother-in-law's face. It was red from the heat and her eyes had dark circles around them. She resolved to perform this laborious task by herself when another supply of soap was needed. Bethiah was becoming too frail for such heavy work. Then she answered, "Yes, it looks good, Mother Wilson. You certainly have a knack for soap making and possess so many other skills as well."

"Just years of hard work and learning from experience, My Dear," replied Bethiah. "You're very capable yourself, especially for one so young, and I don't know what I'd do without you," she added, smiling lovingly at her daughter-in-law.

Their task finished, both women bathed and changed their clothes. Then Harriet made bread dough and put it in a large bowl, covering it with a clean cloth and placed it on the rear of the stove to rise, so that it would be ready to bake for the evening meal. Now with the bread rising and beans simmering in the pot in the oven, Harriet breathed a sigh of relief, grateful to have accomplished so much that day. Now their soap supply was replenished with two dozen nice solid bars, and most of the work for the preparation of the evening meal was finished. Impulsively, she slipped outside again, lying down on the cushiony carpet of the verdant new grass, and savoring the sweetness of the new greenery. When nestling against the fresh scent of her grassy couch, the sun's caressing rays gave her a feeling of well-being, and she absorbed them like a flower raising its face to that golden orb's benevolent touch. While watching its golden glances caressing the tiny buds on the apple trees, she felt the warmth of the earth against her winter weary body. Her spirit was invigorated and the birdsong and scent of spring blossoms permeated her being. During these wonderful times, she immersed herself deeply in the earth's gentle rhythm, which she later translated into melodies on her clavichord and memory paintings with watercolors. Somehow after these quiet times, her brush flowed as though it had a soul of its own into the essences of flowers, such as the wild roses tumbling in pink profusion over the rock pile which stood on the edge of the orchard, or the quiet, misted mountains rising beyond the forest below the meadow. These paintings, which invigorated her spirit, were the most expressive of the creative impulses surging through her being during these moments of profound tranquillity and solitude. Also, while basking in the immensity of God's tremendous gift of nature—more precious and lovelier than any manmade object could be, was one of the instances when she sensed his presence the most profoundly.

Baby squirrels frolicked beside the trees trying to emulate the antics of their parents, who hopped fearlessly from one slender branch to another. The air was permeated with the delicate scent of the budding lilac bushes, Harriet's favorite flower. What a delightful foretaste of spring, she mused. Also, the warming weather meant the logging drive would soon be completed, and her dear husband would stand tall in the doorway. Then the long, lonely months of their separation would dissolve in the sunshine and the song of the returning birds, vanishing into the realm of fading memories. How reluctant Simeon had been to return to the woods to perform logging work yet another winter and to leave Harriet with so much added work along with her already busy household schedule. Joshua and Bethiah were even more frail then they had been the previous winter when he had also been away logging. However, there had been another scant harvest and cash for necessities was again very depleted. As a result, he had no choice but to take advantage of the only employment he found available, and Harriet forced herself to appear cheerful and attempted to hide her fears concerning this dangerous work, especially the logging drives, and did so until he left. Afterwards, she walked outside, hiding herself behind a giant spruce tree and wept.

After momentarily dozing off, she arose quickly, dashing to the kitchen, and was grateful when she arrived in time to punch the bread dough down for its final rising, before it spilled over the top of the bowl. Now it could be shaped into loaves for baking. Supper would be early tonight to allow time for the quilting bee. Matilda, Amy, along with several other ladies, would attend to assist in the stitching of numerous small pieces of material to form small squares, which could later be sewed together, tacked with yarn through its filling and backing to secure the material until the quilting stitching had been completed. Crazy quilts made from squares formed by various random scraps were the easiest to make and took less time than the patterned quilts. Tonight they would be making a quilt in the wedding ring pattern, which consisted of patchwork rings, sewed on the squares, that would be joined together to form the quilt top. They would be presenting it to Lucy Collins, who was getting married in six weeks. The nimble fingers of the ladies gathered around the long kitchen table didn't miss a stitch, even though they worked rapidly. The quilt would be ready in time, even if they had to work by candlelight long into the night, although each of the women had already spent several hours = performing her own daily routine of housework and cooking meals. However, it was a labor of love for Harriet, who preferred making quilts such as these, with pretty designs, which seemed to her almost as though she were painting a picture. She hummed happily, looking forward to the evening's activities, and the company of her neighbors.

CHAPTER 14

▼

SPRING LOVE

Simeon was repairing a harness and when sensing a presence, he looked up and saw Jonathan standing beside him. He could appear suddenly just as he had done now, as noiseless as an approaching Indian. No wonder, mused Simeon after the young man had spent so many years with them. It could be disconcerting at times, even though the Indians Simeon had encountered were friendly and most of them had moved away. Also, he was getting accustomed to Jonathan's quiet approaches. "Is something the matter, Jonathan? You look rather nervous," inquired Simeon.

"Simeon, you know that I don't know much about courting, much less proposing to a girl, growing up among the Indians the way I did. Harriet's always telling me how romantic you are, so I thought maybe you could give me some advice," said Jonathan, his face slightly crimson.

Ordinarily Simeon would have joked around a bit, but aware of how difficult it was for Jonathan, shy in matters of the heart, he got right to the point. "You want to propose to Amy, don't you, Jon?"

"Have my feelings for her been that obvious?"

"Of course, and hers as well. All anyone has to do is to watch your faces any time when you are together."

"Do you think it is too soon after her losing Ben?

"No, it has been over a year now since Ben was killed during that logging drive.

She needs to start a new life for herself and little Ben now. Ben would want that."

"Do you really think that she might care for me a little?"

"Of course, you have been there for her and little Ben ever since the tragedy. You caught her in your arms when she fainted after hearing the sad news and you have done everything you could for both of them ever since."

"But I don't want her gratitude. I want her love."

"I'm sure that you have it, Jon."

"Then how do I ask her to marry me?"

First your slick yourself up and dress in your Sunday best and I don't mean those worn deerskin clothes you have. Get a nice suit of clothes. Then get down on one knee and tell her that you love her and want her to be your wife more than anything else in the world."

"Is that the way you proposed to Harriet?"

"Yes, and I meant it and I am sure that you do as well."

"What if I get so nervous that I forget what to say?"

"Then let your heart speak. That is really what I did. I was just as nervous as you are," answered Simeon.

Before he lost his courage, Jonathan hurried down to Mosby's general store and was amazed to find a suit in stock which fit him perfectly. The formal clothing made from expensive fabric seemed odd to him after dressing so informally for so many years, and although he expected the suit to feel restricting and uncomfortable, was happily surprised to find that it provided sufficient ease of movement. He looked at his reflection in the store mirror and mused, with a little hair trim and a shave, I might look rather presentable.

After a visit to the barber, and another look at himself in the mirror, his courage was bolstered just enough to approach his lovely Amy. He found her outside behind the house attempting to spade up a vegetable patch. Her blue cotton dress was splashed with mud and her hair, black as a river, had fallen out of its pins in the spring breezes. She had never looked lovelier to him.

"My heart's treasure," he blurted, "Why didn't you leave that spading for me to do. You know I had planned to attend to it."

"But I accept so much help from you," she answered and then asked "Jonathan, what did you just call me?"

Jonathan slyly repeated, "My heart's treasure, Amy, because that's what you are." And then, before he lost his courage, he got down on his knee on the muddy ground in his new suit and blurted, "Amy, could you possibly care for me enough to marry me? I love you with every fiber of my being. I know I can never take

Ben's place, nor do I expect to, but if I could have just a little corner of your heart."

"You can have much more than a corner, Jonathan. I love you too. I didn't know whether you cared for me or just felt sorry for me. That's why I started digging my garden so I wouldn't be a burden to you if you only felt pity. You are such a kind loving person, I just didn't know. Ben would have wanted me to remarry. He wouldn't have wished for me to spend my life alone. He was that kind of person. Yes, Jonathan, my Darling, I will marry you whenever you want me to."

At that moment, all Jonathan's shyness disappeared and he took the woman he adored in his arms and kissed her tenderly, murmuring, "How about Saturday? The circuit preacher will be at our church then."

Amy reached up, threw her arms around him, returning his kisses and with her face radiant answered, "Yes, my dear, I will marry you then if you don't mind a rather shabby bride. There won't be much time to get a new dress," she added laughing.

Then she looked in consternation at her soiled clothing and touched her loose disheveled hair. "Oh, I look a fright, and you look as handsome as a prince in your fine clothes, all except for your muddy knees," she added laughing.

"You are the loveliest sight I have ever seen, and I don't care if your wear a burlap bag to our wedding, as long as you're there to marry me." Then he held her close again, and the spring song of the birds and the soft breezes rustling through the new green leaves of the trees added their voices to the symphony in his heart.

Amy and Jonathan stood together blissfully clasped in one another's arms, until little Ben, awakened from his nap, rushed out to greet them. Then Jonathan remained outside to play ball with the small child who would soon become his stepson, while Amy changed into fresh clothing. However, just before the couple left to tell Harriet and Simeon the happy news, he suddenly remembered that in his excitement concerning their upcoming marriage, he had forgotten to mention his purchase the previous day of the house and land from Richard Payne. Jonathan had used a portion of the inheritance which his mother's brother, Samuel, had left him, to buy the property. His uncle had spent years searching for his missing nephew, and his hope had been rekindled when he learned that Jonathan's body hadn't been found with those of his parents. Finally, a few months before Samuel's death, his lawyer was able to contact Jonathan after Harriet had posted a letter to her mother, Elizabeth, containing the news of his return, and recollection of his identity after 12 years of amnesia Immediately afterwards, she contacted her brother-in-law, who had written previously seeking knowledge of his nephew's whereabouts, to relate Harriet's good news concerning his long lost relative. After a joyful reunion with Jonathan, Samuel decided to leave him half of his estate, and the remainder would be given to his surviving brother, Ezekiel.

Jonathan was forced to act quickly in his purchase of the property, because Richard Payne was moving his family to the fertile, inexpensive lands of Ohio. Weary of wresting a living from the rocky New England soil, he was convinced to head west after his brother Dan, who had migrated to Ohio just a year ago, had written describing its rich soil and his flourishing crops of corn, wheat, barley, and vegetables as well as a climate much more compatible to farming than that of New England's. In his recent letter, he stated, "It's so easy to till the soil in this place that a small child could do it." After Richard's decision was finally made to leave, he needed cash quickly for his trip. Jonathan, impressed with the 100 acres of partially cleared land, abundant with wild blueberries, which he planned to market in Bangor and Ellsworth, and the two story, frame house already built, quickly bought the property. Not knowing at the time whether Amy would consider leaving her home, in retrospect Jonathan wished that he had asked for her opinion before the purchase had been made.

When Amy entered the room, little Ben was straddling the back of the young man, who was soon to become her husband, attired in his newly purchased clothes on his hands and knees pretending to be a horse.

"Jonathan! Whatever am I to do with you? Look what you're doing to your new suit. If you persist in behaving this manner, we shall both have to get married wearing burlap bags," she said laughing. Then her eyes almost filled with tears, because it was so obvious when observing the pair that Jonathan would be a wonderful father for her small son. She had never believed it would be possible to ever experience so much happiness again and with this gentle, kind man, who was quite different from Ben, but wonderful in his unique way. Then she noticed his troubled expression, and asked, "Darling, you know I was only teasing, don't you? You look a little upset."

"Of course, my love," he answered, "It's just that I should have asked your opinion about the property I just bought before purchasing it. I'm wondering now if you can bear to leave your home you have struggled so desperately to keep to come and share my house with me. If not, I will sell it and stay here with you."

"Oh, my dearest, of course I will be happy to live with you wherever you wish me to. Even in a dugout or a shack. Any home will be a palace with you there to love me," replied Amy, reaching up to hug him.

"What a relief," he murmured, his lips brushing her hair. "It is the Payne property."

"The Payne property! That is one of the nicest houses in town. Why would they want to leave it and did you find gold somewhere?," she added.

"Richard heard about the easily tilled soil and inexpensive land in Ohio from his brother, Dan. Remember when he moved there last year? As for the gold mine, I received an inheritance from my uncle a month or so ago. It enabled me to buy some property, and a threshold to carry my bride over," he answered holding her close.

Of course, Jonathan mused, Amy would have responded agreeably, because since the day that he had begun looking after the grieving young widow, she had made him feel as though he were as wise as a sage and trusted his wisdom in any decision which had to be made regarding her welfare and that of her little son. Amy also understood his reluctance to hunt, which was not only a way of life among all the men of the village to obtain food for the tables of their families, but to establish themselves as good providers as well. As soon as a boy could manage a rifle, he was taught to shoot. Even though during his life with the Indians, he was taught to use the bow and arrow, but was never forced to hunt. The Indians, themselves, although they hunted for food, used every part of the animal, wasting nothing, and even asked permission from them to take their lives for their own sustenance. Jonathan respected them for this and also because they showed him how to use nuts, roots, and beans in place of meat. Amy had once told him, sobbing because she had never appreciated Ben's hunting prowess and had disappointed him one day when he had come home filled with pride because he had killed a rabbit for their evening meal by crying, and pitying the animal so much she couldn't bear to dress it. At that point in her grieving process, Amy, just as many who have lost a loved one do, had allowed all the things she had felt she had let Ben down in, flow through her psyche. At that point, Jonathan had shyly held her and because it was so soon after she had lost Ben, felt guilt permeating those stirrings within him for this lovely young woman, who made him feel virile and manly, despite his nonconformity to the regular male role as a hunter, which was expected of him especially as a frontiersman. Even as close as he was to Harriet and Simeon, neither could understand his hatred of hunting nor his vegetarian ways, although they didn't ridicule him for this such as most other townspeople did, especially the young girl who had called him a pantywaist. But, Amy, his Amy, loved him just as he was He caressed her hair, dark as a raven's wing, found the sweetness of her lips again and then reluctantly, released her and the three of them climbed into his wagon to visit Harriet and Simeon and to tell them their joyful news.

CHAPTER 15

▼

WEDDING

Immediately after hearing about Jonathan and Amy's coming marriage, Harriet and Matilda joined the bride to be in her efforts to make a suitable gown during the one day remaining before the marriage would take place. Because of the limited time period, instead of measuring Amy to construct a pattern, Harriet carefully took apart the seams of one of the girl's threadbare dresses and laid it over the shimmering cream colored silk Matilda had provided as a wedding present, cutting it a bit fuller in the skirt than the original garment, to allow enough material for soft gathers just below the bust line, in order to fashion it in the empire style initiated by the Empress Josephine, wife of Napoleon. Amy, Matilda, and Harriet sat around the fireplace utilizing both the light provided by the small blaze which had been lit because of the chilly dampness of the rainy spring evening, as well as the light of several candles for their sewing of the dress, until Harriet shooed the bride to be off, so she would look fresh for her wedding. Also, she finally convinced Matilda, who had shown considerable reluctance to leave her alone to finish their task which required several hours yet to complete, that expectant mothers needed their rest and to go home to do so. Harriet laid her needle down just as the pale gold rays of the morning sun glittered through the lace of the parlor curtains. She stretched her tired muscles for a moment, and then gazed happily at the sunlit skies, grateful that Amy and Jonathan would have such pleasant weather for their wedding. Afterwards, she held the finished gown up for inspection, and smiled with satisfaction. It had turned out well. She could just picture a radiant Amy, in the pretty dress, made with loving care and material of excellent quality, which would hang gracefully around the young woman's girlish figure.

After an invigorating cup of coffee and a thick slice of Bethiah's sourdough bread, she made breakfast for her awakened family and then hurried to show the finished wedding garment to Matilda, so that she could see how beautifully the material she had provided made up, and then dashed out to deliver it to an ecstatic Amy. When Harriet presented her with the lovely, finished dress, Amy's eyes filled with tears of gratitude and wonder. It was difficult to believe that this perfectly constructed garment could have been produced in such a short span of time. Hugging first Harriet and then Matilda, she murmured, "You two have given me a gown which is fit for a princess! I never dreamed of ever owning such a lovely wedding dress. I was joking with Jonathan after he proposed about having to wear a burlap bag to be married in."

After Amy took her beautiful gown, carrying it as if it were made of pure gold to place on a hanger, she hugged the two women again saying, "I can never thank you enough."

"It was a labor of love," replied Harriet. "Now shoo, and get ready for your wedding. We'll take little Ben home with us so you can do so without any interruptions."

Later, after the children were napping, Bethiah volunteered to watch them while Harriet and Matilda got together with all the other ladies in town to prepare the remainder of the food needed for the party they had planned for the newlyweds. Amazingly, even though time was limited, an impromptu feast was ready, spread out on the long rectangular tables which the townspeople utilized for whatever events in which they should be needed, just moments before the couple entered the church for the ceremony. It consisted of cold roast beef, baked macaroni and cheese, stuffed eggs, fresh baked crusty rolls, peach, apple, custard tarts, lemonade, tea, and a delectable wedding cake which was topped with snowy white icing and decorated with a colorful ring of sweet peas. Harriet fashioned a bouquet for the bride from the wild lilac bushes behind the house, and also picked some more to adorn the food covered tables which were spread out under the luxurious foliage of the maple grove behind the little white church.

After the ceremony when the newlyweds began to climb up into Jonathan's newly purchased buggy, amid hugs, kisses and congratulations, Simeon intercepted them to lead the astonished couple behind the Church for their surprise wedding reception. Almost all of the inhabitants of the little hamlet were there and most of them had contributed something for the feast. Not only were Amy and Jonathan loved by many of the neighbors, but also, weddings gave these hard working folks an occasion for celebration and fun, which was a welcome respite from their usual laborious schedules.

CHAPTER 16

▼

CHILDREN'S TIME

It was 1826 and John Quincy Adams, who had been Secretary of State under James Monroe, the previous president, now took the helm as the country's new leader. Joshua's opinion was that Adams appeared to be a good, knowledgeable man, but after the many accomplishments of his predecessor, he would have a lot to live up to. One thing in particular, was the former president's establishment of the Monroe Doctrine. Since Joshua had fought for his country in the Revolutionary War, he was particularly happy about the part of the doctrine which deterred European colonization in the Americas.

He commented, "We have worked too hard to settle this country to have other nations come over and take over bits and pieces of our lands. Not to mention the many wars we have gone through with all the pillaging and burning of towns and cities just about as soon as they were built up."

In 1803 when Monroe had been Secretary of State under President Thomas Jefferson, who sent him, along Robert Livingston, to purchase Louisiana from France, he played an important role in the negotiations. This acquisition provided the United States, then a fledgling country, with a large tract of land containing almost a million acres, abundant with rich natural resources. Although the purchase was Jefferson's idea, Monroe was already showing his expertise in handling matters of great importance to his nation and had served it well throughout his presidency.

So many of the tremendous changes in this young country of ours had occurred in such a short span of time, Harriet mused. Even in their remote little hamlet, they had hired their own school teacher for the rapidly increasing number of students in their one room schoolhouse. Miss Prentice was a tall, elegant looking woman, with her abundance of silvery hair pinned up to frame her rather austere countenance, which belied her genuine warmth and caring for all of her pupils. For those who knew her well, it was actually a façade to provide discipline in the classroom. She took a personal interest in each of her students and attempted to bring into fruition their individual talents. Miss Prentice possessed her own horse and buggy despite the miniscule salary provided during her many years of teaching. This, along with her confident manner, made her appear as a woman of an independent nature and also a good role model for all her students, especially girls with little self confidence. She boarded with Matilda and Albert utilizing their spare room. Great Pond's population had risen to 150 and the little school now had thirty students. Also, the changing attitude of the parents, who valued at least some degree of basic education for both sons and daughters, either relinquished a portion of their chores or rearranged schedules of those which they performed, enabling the children to attend school. Previously, only the sons were the ones who were encouraged to pursue higher education, but many changes were taking place concerning the females' roles in society. In the past, it was not uncommon to hear a father state, "My girls will not need an education, because they will marry and their husbands will support them, so my boys are the ones who need the schooling." Of course at the time, some of the people hadn't taken into consideration that perhaps a daughter might not wed or become widowed, and providing her with an good education would be advantageous in obtaining a position which would provide enough income to enable her to obtain a reasonable standard of living. Even though many enterprising women, though single, did manage to support themselves by opening their homes to boarders or even starting some type of business venture, formal training certainly would have given them greater occupational opportunities, especially in the teaching field. Fortunately at the present time, more thought had been given to the daughters' education and many young women were presently enrolled in academies and seminaries. Emma Willard, born in Connecticut in 1787, was a remarkable woman who demonstrated a passionate concern for the education of women, had opened a seminary for girls in Troy, New York, in 1821, after having previously founded a female seminary in Middlebury, Vermont in 1814. Also, there was Bradford Academy, founded in 1803, several miles closer to home which accepted both sexes. While reflecting upon the emerging awareness of the importance of educational opportunities for women, Harriet pondered wistfully about the possibility of her daughters attending a school of higher learning. Perhaps someday all my children can have a good education, she murmured to herself Although Harriet had little formal education, her mother had taught her reading, writing, and arithmetic by the time she was seven, and at the age of ten, she had learned to play the clavichord as well as painting with water colors. Since that time, Harriet devoured every book available to expand her education and this was fulfilling to her.

Even though it had been just a half century since the United States had won its independence, Harriet reflected, some incredible events were taking place. People were migrating to Texas, which seemed almost unbelievable to her, because this huge state was so many miles away. In 1821, it had just become a part of Mexico, and the Spanish had given permission for settlers to come to farm, plant or trade, and to pursue their dreams in the large territory available. Just six years ago in 1820, the population of the United States had risen from the 1790 population of about 4,000,000 to an astounding figure of 9,632,403! Harriet was astonished. So much had happened in such a short span of time.

Where had the past five years flown? Harriet mused. It seemed incredible that so much time had elapsed since the family had made the trip by ox cart from New Brunswick to make their home with Simeon's aging parents. At that time little Jamie had not yet been born, and he was now four years of age. Her thoughts about him were interrupted suddenly when he entered the room, tears streaming down his little, dirt streaked face.

"What's the matter, my darling little Jamie?" asked Harriet, pulling his sweaty little body close while she hugged him comfortingly.

"I didn't fill the basket with blueberries like you asked me to, Mama," he sobbed. "Now you won't be able to make pie." Then, sheepishly he admitted, "I ate most of them."

Jennie, now six, placed her arm around him and said, "But, Mama, he is just a little boy, and he didn't mean to eat so many."

Harriet smiled, musing at the motherliness of her small daughter, just two years older than her brother, yet already attempting to protect him.

"I'm not going to punish him, dear," she answered. "It was a large basket for a little boy to fill, and those juicy blueberries were pretty tempting, especially on such a hot day. With the ones Jamie had remaining in his basket and yours, I think that I can manage to make a nice big blueberry cake. Would you both like that?" she asked when leaning down to hug them.

"Oh yes, Mama," they replied in unison, and while bestowing his kisses of gratitude, Jamie added a little smudge to Harriet's face in the process.

Harriet couldn't believe how quickly her children were growing up. Simeon Jr., whom they called Simmy, now seven, helped his father with many of the chores, such as pitching hay and feeding grain to the livestock. Another task he performed was keeping the wood box well supplied with the seasoned maple, oak, and birch split into compact stove size pieces, which provided steady heat, and was not only the best wood for baking, but provided the most warmth as well. This particular receptacle had a lid opening in the shed to the left of the door which led to the kitchen, and another inside, providing an arrangement which was not only beneficial in keeping the cold drafts of winter from cooling off the kitchen, but was convenient as well, for whoever replenished the wood in the kitchen range.

Pitching hay had recently become one of Simmy's tasks, because his father had just decided that his oldest son understood how dangerous this implement might be if extreme caution wasn't practiced in its use. Also, Harriet realized that Simeon had given him this added responsibility because he considered the child mature for his age as all their children appeared to be. Simmy's dark, wavy hair and deep blue eyes were so similar to his father's that Harriet pictured him as a little miniature of his paternal parent when he had been the same age. During these quiet moments of contemplation, Harriet's thoughts drifted to Jennie, who could already knit a warm scarf, and had started a pair of mittens as well as a sampler. At the moment, she was eagerly employing her small hands by assisting her grandmother in braiding heavy strips of wool cut from worn garments, which were utilized to make cozy rugs to adorn the wide boarded floors. She also sewed quilt patches together to form small squares with stitches almost as perfect as her mother's, and the child's competent work substantially hastened the quilting process for Bethiah and Harriet. Along with these other tasks, Jennie dusted as well. Jennie resembled Harriet with her small boned little body and red gold hair, but her eye color was the same deep blue as her father's rather than that of her mother's, whose were of a velvety brown hue. Harriet bent down to brush a caress against her daughter's cheek, while musing about how much her little girl eased her work load while she attended to all the responsibilities involved in caring for her rapidly growing family.

Harriet, although not desiring to keep her little daughter too busy to enjoy being a child, merely taught her how to attend to the same chores and needlework skills in which her own mother had instructed her to perform at the same age. Elizabeth, five, assisted with the dusting and had begun a sampler. Little

Jamie loved to help as well, so his job was feeding the chickens and gathering eggs. Jamie also had his mother's red god hair and brown eyes, but instead of her petite frame, was a rugged, large boned child resembling Harriet's youngest brother, Peter. Elizabeth resembled her grandmother, for whom she was named, fine featured with hair the same raven black shade as hers had been before it turned silver and as well as the same hazel eye color.

Even though Harriet's days were always filled with numerous household tasks and many other activities, she took time each afternoon to spend with her children, giving them her undivided attention. She read to them, they sang together gathered around the little clavichord which her grandmother had given her for her twelfth birthday, and also took time to listen to each child's concerns.

In the evenings during the week, after the daily chores were done, Harriet and Simeon gathered around the fireplace and each child approaching school age was taught the alphabet and multiplication tables through 12 x 12. Each new baby was a welcome addition to their growing family, and one day while Harriet was relaxing in her favorite chair, after her usual afternoon time with her children, musing about how blessed she was to have such a wonderful family, she felt the familiar fluttering, light as the touch of a butterfly's wings, of the first communication from the tiny new life within her. She smiled, brushing a wayward strand of hair away from her forehead and decided that if this child were a girl, she would be the namesake of Bethiah, her beloved mother-in-law. If the child were a boy, his name would be Joshua after her dear father-in-law. While she sat basking in her anticipation of a new baby, her reverie was suddenly interrupted by the chimes of the faithful old grandfather clock in the parlor, announcing it was time to prepare the evening meal. Refreshed and energized by her time with her children, she quickly arose from her comfortable chair to prepare the family meal. After the whole house was permeated with the scent of the juicy, blueberry cake she had promised, she set it on the top of the kitchen range to cool, and then replenished the stove with more of the carefully split and sized pieces of hardwood. This type of wood, usually yellow birch or maple, burned more slowly and provided an even heat and the high temperature required in order to bake the flaky melt-in-your-mouth biscuits which Harriet had made. Since the cake needed a lower baking temperature than the biscuits, the oven would have to gain the necessary heat needed for them to be light and evenly browned. She hummed contentedly as she placed the hearty, leftover stew towards the rear of the stove to keep it warm and took out her bread board and rolling pin, assembled the ingredients for making the biscuits, and then kneaded the soft, pliable dough until it was light and puffy. Then Harriet rolled it out on the large board Joshua had made, sprinkling it with flour and cutting it out into twenty four uniform pieces, with the generously sized, round biscuit cutter Bethiah had brought from Taunton. Making less than two-dozen biscuits would be a waste of time, she mused, while popping the large, flat sheet into the oven.

Soon the delicate aroma of the baking and the meat and vegetable stew filled the whole house. "Good, supper will be a little early," she murmured, "There will be plenty of time for our meal and to get the dishes washed before the Sing tonight." Every Wednesday evening, the neighbors came to sing, gathering around in the parlor while while Harriet accompanied them on her clavichord. This activity rekindled memories of her home in New Brunswick, because her mother had entertained her neighbors in the family home for Sings as well. She smiled, her face glowing with the fond memories of those happy times, and was glad that the people in her new home enjoyed singing as much as her Fredericton neighbors had These Wednesday night Sings provided a little break in the week for people who worked hard and also had few opportunities for recreation. They sang the old familiar songs and hymns, which they had sung since childhood, and everyone took part in the singing, whether off key or in tune. Wednesday night was eagerly anticipated and provided a rejuvenating release for all. They came summer and winter, despite the weather, rubbing moisture from their brows in the hot weather with their handkerchiefs, or with snow sparkling in their hair on a wintry evening, young and old alike. Harriet smiled, thinking about how this fun filled time made her children so happy, not only because they loved to sing, but because they also had the privilege of staying up an hour later during these evening gatherings.

When the village folks arrived, the aroma of Harriet's baking still lingered throughout the house, giving it a warm, cozy atmosphere. Amy and Jonathan, and little Ben arrived first, and then the others came, eager to have some recreation after their long day's labors. Almost immediately the parlor was filled with exuberant voices and the music of the old clavichord. Harriet marveled while tired faces were illuminated with childlike joy, and the weariness of their long arduous days were lifted by the music and singing. She smiled in remembrance of her former faraway home in New Brunswick, and never had she felt as much at home in her present one.

CHAPTER 17

▼

STRUGGLES

Simeon's fever hadn't broken, and Joshua's old hip wound ached during the damp, stormy weather, which there had been so much of lately, so both men were unable to perform their usual chores. As a result, Simmy and Harriet were doing their best to keep the animals fed and watered, the cows milked, and when the supply of stove ready wood was needed, to chop more to replenish it.

"It is already the 31st of January. Hopefully the coldest part of the winter is past there will be a February thaw soon which will bring us some warmer weather. Then perhaps Papa Joshua's hip won't hurt him so much, and it would also be helpful to Simeon in getting over his cold." Harriet commented to Bethiah as she applied onion poultices to Simeon's chest to break the congestion in his lungs.

"I hope so, Child," answered Bethiah, "We surely could use a break in this miserable weather. Also, I feel so bad that you and little Simmy have so much extra work on your shoulders. I worry about you, especially, being in the family way again and your baby due any day now," she added, her kind eyes filled with concern.

"Don't worry about us, Mother Williams. We are both strong and healthy and some extra chores won't hurt us," Harriet replied. Then she patted her loving mother-in-law's shoulder gently, and while brushing a kiss on her cheek, murmured, "I couldn't perform any of these duties without your help with the housework and the children. Your own work load is heavier than ever."

After giving Bethiah a reassuring hug, she pulled on a pair of Simeon's heavy wool stockings, and slipped into his high boots. Although her husband's feet were small for a man's, it was still necessary to stuff the toes of the boots with rags to keep them from falling off. She donned his heavy coat, tied a wool scarf around her head, and went out to make her way through the storm to feed and water the hungry, thirsty animals and chickens. Icy needles struck her face, and the wind almost threw her into waist high drifts, but stubbornly she shoveled just enough of the heavy banked snow along its fifty feet distance between the house and the barn to push through to her destination. During her ordeal, she momentarily regretted the family decision to build the structure so far away from the other buildings, instead of connecting them all to the house as many of the neighbors had done. Their fear had been, in case of fire that everything would burn. When a fire started in this isolated hamlet, especially in winter, which significantly hampered their efforts to obtain assistance quickly, there would be little hope of saving anything. Even though there was a volunteer fire department with fast horses in Aurora, just six miles away, after they were summoned and had arrived, it would be too late. Of course all the neighbors would rush to assist them, but unfortunately, the well was their only source of water nearby. If it were frozen over, it would take extra time to break the ice. Also, a few pails of water, not to mention the time it took to draw it up from the well added to the problem and the nearest pond was almost a mile away, so building the barn a safe distance away from the house was the most practical thing to do. At least the animals would be saved and it would provide a place for the family to stay until better living arrangements could be made.

When Harriet finally reached the barn, Bessie was already in pain, because it was an hour past her usual milking time, so she decided to milk her before watering and feeding the other animals and the chickens. She took the pail off its hook on wall which was located near the animal's stall and seated herself on the milking stool, grateful for the warmth of the cow's body, while the rich streams of liquid filled the bucket. The stable was divided off from the wide expanse of the barn, as was the chicken house, which was across from it on the left side of the spacious building. Her milking finished, Harriet reluctantly left the shelter of the barn carrying two water buckets to cut down on her trips back and forth from the well as she made her way through the snow. Winding the long rope down the rock lined well with the crank, she was grateful to find that the pail filled with water instead of striking ice. After several trips, the watering was finished, and she pitched hay into the mangers of the horse and cow, as well as scattering dry corn for the chickens. Then after cleaning the stalls and scattering fresh straw in them, she was free to battle her way through the intensifying storm with the fruits of her labors, frothy, creamy milk and a dozen fresh eggs. In the summer there would have been a larger quantity of milk and eggs, but hens didn't lay as much in the winter and the cow's milk gradually dried up before freshening after the birth of a spring calf.

The moment Harriet reached the door, the welcoming warmth of the kitchen was permeated with a delicious aroma of something baking, and Bethiah helped her off with her half frozen outer garments, saying "Land sakes, Child, You look like a walking snow man." Then she pulled a chair close to the stove for the exhausted young woman, covering her with a wooly blanket, and presented her with a plate containing two large, fluffy biscuits, straight from the oven, slathered with creamy butter, along with a steaming cup of tea, brewed until it was red, just the way Harriet liked it. The warmth of the teacup felt soothing to her hands which stung from the cold, and the hot biscuits tasted better than anything she could remember having eaten. After finishing Bethiah's welcome treat, Harriet noticed Joshua, with an agonized expression on his face, sitting forlornly in his rocking chair, drawn close to the oven door, which had been left open after the baking was finished to utilize its remaining heat. She sensed immediately that he felt old and helpless, while once again his pregnant daughter-in-law performed a task he no longer had the physical ability to attend to, especially in a blizzard such as this one. Her heart ached for him and she wondered what it would be like when she too grew elderly and couldn't manage the chores she was so accustomed to performing. She sighed, pushing a wet strand of hair from her forehead.

The next day dawned with temperatures twenty degrees warmer than the previous morning's, and the bright winter sun sprinkled the snow with glittering crystals, as if it were an apologetic token for the harsh weather of the previous day. Soon after breakfast had been served and the dishes were washed and put away, Jonathan and Amy arrived in their high-backed sleigh, apologetic for not having been there for assistance during the blizzard, after Joshua inadvertently told them of Harriet's performing the chores during the storm. Then she replied smiling, "How could you have known that Simeon was so ill? Anyway, you know that I'm strong and healthy."

"Nevertheless, I should have checked," answered Jonathan. "You shouldn't be doing heavy work in your condition. We did have a special reason not to venture out yesterday. Do you want to tell them, My Love," Jonathan said, his face almost as radiant as the sun's while gazing lovingly at his wife.

"I'm going to have a child, as well," Amy replied. "We're ecstatic!"

Both Harriet and Bethiah attempted not to show their concern while remembering the difficult birth of Little Ben. Perhaps her second child will come more easily, they reasoned, both saying a silent prayer. Both women quickly decided not to inform the expectant father about Amy's problems while bearing little Ben. By doing so, it would not only cause him great distress, but there was nothing he could do about it except worry. Quickly they hugged and congratulated the happy couple convincingly, and celebrated their joyful news, utilizing the expensive imported tea, which Matilda's father had presented them with for Christmas.

That night, just as the old clock in the parlor struck twelve, Bethiah delivered Harriet's fifth child, a strong, nine pound boy, which as planned was named, Joshua. His grandfather's joy with his little namesake momentarily transformed his face into that of the visage of a much younger man, erasing its tiredness, and replacing it with youthful exuberance. He eagerly took the newborn into his arms, with tears of joy cascading down his cheeks. Despite her heavy workload during Harriet's pregnancy and the size of baby, she bore him easily. After awakening from a sound sleep, she found that she was almost ready to be delivered

Five months later, on a cloudless, balmy summer day, Jonathan raced up to the door after driving his buggy as fast as the horse could run, his face as white with concern as Amy's first husband's had been during her ordeal in giving birth to Little Ben. After quickly assembling to the needed herbs and clean linens, Harriet climbed into the buggy with Jonathan, her heart pounding with anxiety. Bethiah was too frail at this point to assist, leaving Harriet without the assistance and expertise of the older woman whose many years of midwifery had subjected her to such a variety of childbirths, including many of a difficult nature. Although her own experience as a midwife was now considerable, she longed for Bethiah to be there with her. Not only for her superior skills, should there be problems with the birthing, but also for the comforting presence of the woman who had become so much like a mother to her. Harriet murmured a quick prayer, which assisted in calming her and in taking charge of her emotions, because not only did she need to appear confident and unworried, for Amy's welfare, but for Jonathan's as well.

They arrived at the couple's home almost as speedily as Jonathan had when coming to fetch her, because Simeon had quickly hooked up his own horse to the buggy to give his worried friend's exhausted animal a rest. Harriet managed a confident smile while entering the house to attend to Amy. Instead of the screams following each searing pain, which she encountered when Amy was bearing little Ben, everything was silent. Fearing the worst, she dashed into the room, and when Harriet looked at the bed where Amy was lying, the happy young mother smiled, and said, "You have arrived just in time to cut the cord. My little daughter was born very quickly and almost without pain!"

Tears of both joy and the release from her fears concerning Amy's safe delivery of her little girl, rained down Harriet's cheeks, while she said a quick prayer of thanks. After rapidly regaining her composure, she attended to the umbilical cord and bathed both Amy and the lively, perfectly formed little child. Afterwards, she changed the bed utilizing the fresh linens she had brought with her. Then she placed the baby, wrapped in the soft, fluffy blanket she had made as a present for the infant, in her mother's arms, while the exuberant young father caressed his wife. His tears of both exuberance and relief unashamedly fell against his cheek while he gently embraced her.

After a few incredulous moments, Harriet asked, "Amy, why didn't you send for me earlier?"

"Because my preliminary pains were so much milder than those which I had experienced when I gave birth to little Ben, I didn't realize that I was already in the last stages of labor when I asked Jonathan to fetch you," replied Amy.

"Oh, my dear friend," Harriet answered, while leaning down to caress Amy's cheek, "I am so glad that you didn't have to…" and then quickly she realized that she had almost told Jonathan about Amy's previous, intense suffering, and then continued, "wait long for your precious baby to arrive."

Later, after the happy young mother had been given a nice cup of tea and a thick slice of toast made from a loaf of bread Bethiah had baked that morning, Harriet heated some stew Amy had prepared the day before for Jonathan, and after he had eaten, she placed the new father's tiny daughter in his arms. Harriet's face again was streaked with tears when she saw the love and awe illuminating Jonathan's face. Now the family of the young man who had been orphaned so tragically at twelve, not only consisted of a loving wife, a stepson he adored, but his own little daughter as well

CHAPTER 18

▼

ELIZABETH'S DECISION

Elizabeth was growing increasingly more restless each day. So many changes had taken place in her life since her dear husband, Ezra, had passed away eight years ago, so unexpectedly one evening. He had been stricken with a congestion in his chest and was ill for a few days, but during the evening before he died, had appeared to feel much better and had even joined the family in singing hymns after their nightly Bible reading. Also, the doctor had called in the previous day and had said Ezra's breathing was no longer labored and that his health was improving rapidly. Elizabeth was completely unaware that what had appeared to have been an ordinary chest cold would result in an ailment as serious as walking pneumonia, which the doctor later diagnosed as Ezra's illness. Elizabeth would carry guilt heavy as a boulder, weighing down her heart, because she felt that she might have been able to save his life had she asked the doctor to check on him again that evening, even though it had appeared as if all the congestion had cleared and his health seemed so much improved. Also, he had assured her he was just fine, although a bit tired and had decided to retire early. Then two hours later, after Elizabeth slipped into her nightgown and started to get into bed, she found him lying there, appearing so calm and peaceful as if he had drifted off into a deep sleep. After her tragic loss, Elizabeth threw her substantial energies into assisting in the care of her grandchildren and with church work. During the past year she had turned down two proposals of marriage from lonely widowers, because somehow she could not bring herself to remarry. Possibly remarriage was impossible for her at the present time, Elizabeth reasoned—perhaps it might be because she couldn't expose herself to the risk of the possibility of out living another husband. Also, lingering shadows of guilt permeated her being and little voices in her psyche such as "If I had called the doctor again or taken better care of him" prolonged her grieving process.

Elizabeth had turned her eight-room house over to her oldest son, Josiah, and his wife Margaret, except for one bedroom which she reserved for herself. Her daughter Betsey and her husband, Charles, had moved to Oromocto to take up residence in his family home soon after Harriet had left for Maine. Three months later, her sons, Samuel and Henry, along with their wives and children had followed them and within a year, built houses of their own. At this point, Josiah and Margaret's family was expanding rapidly. Her daughter-in-law had just borne her sixth child, and they were cramped for space. Elizabeth had never felt that her presence was a burden to the young family, in fact she always helped Margaret with the household chores and in caring for the children, but nevertheless, she felt that the course of her life must be changed. When the letter arrived from Susan Bennett, Margaret's mother, who had just been widowed and whose house had recently burned when struck by lightning, asking if it would be possible for her to move in with her daughter and husband, Elizabeth's decision was made. She would go to her Harriet. It was now 1831, and almost ten years had passed since she had seen her beloved daughter, who was expecting her sixth child in less than two months. Both she and Simeon had begged her many times throughout the years to come and make her home with them. Bethiah and Joshua had slipped away in their sleep just a year ago. Each one's heart had simply stopped, just a month of one another after their long, hardworking lifetimes. Elizabeth would be needed there now and Simeon had just finished off two additional bedrooms upstairs, so there would be plenty of room for her. As quickly as she could arrange passage, she would take the steamship to Bangor and the remainder of the journey could be made by stagecoach. Her trip would be so much more comfortable than Harriet's and Simeon's trek through the wilderness in that oxcart! Finally Elizabeth would not only be reunited with her daughter, but would finally meet the grand children she had never seen. With her heart as light as a girl's, she wrote a letter to Harriet, informing her of when to expect her arrival.

Following much consideration of the matter, Elizabeth told the other members of the family her plans, whose feelings were mixed—happy that she would finally be reunited with their sister after so many years, but sad that she would be such a distance away from them. Elizabeth sighed with relief after she had managed to tell them of her decision. However, although ecstatic because she would soon be with Harriet, a foretaste of the loneliness she would soon experience for the family she was leaving behind, surged through her being. It would be difficult to leave the home where all her children had been born and also, it was the place she had spent so many happy years with her beloved Ezra. He had brought her to the house as a bride, beaming with joy and pride because he had built a comfortable home for her. Sometimes, after losing him, she felt comforted just touching the walls caressingly, because his hands had built them, and it was as though it were a kind of communication with him. Oh, these walls, she mused, they hold the voices and laughter of my children, family celebrations, and the loving communications of a couple wed for thirty two years. Tears rained down her cheeks, which she wiped away quickly with the corner of her apron. She sighed, and after a few more moments of reflection, determinedly plunged into the sentimental chore of sorting her belongings into separate piles—those which would be taken with her and the ones to be left behind. During the first half hour of her task, she transferred objects back and forth from one heap to the other. It appeared that everything she touched represented precious memories. Finally, Elizabeth resolutely took control of her emotions and decided to leave all of her furniture except for her cedar chest, which contained a quilt having been fashioned by utilizing salvaged pieces of all of the family's worn out clothing, a few samplers, crocheted and tatted doilies crafted by her girls, some little animals carved by her boys, and a beautiful, carved picture frame made by her beloved Ezra which contained their marriage certificate. Then she filled a small trunk with her clothing, bed linens, and other personal belongings. There would be no need for bedroom furniture, because the newly constructed room, which would be hers, already contained a lovely maple bedstead and dresser, as well as a chest of drawers, that Joshua had made utilizing his expertise as a carpenter and cabinetmaker. Wistfully, Elizabeth gazed around the room she and Ezra had shared for such a long time, and at the bed in which she had borne all of her children, with its crocheted spread she had fashioned during evenings when sitting around the fireside with her husband, while he mended harnesses, whittled small pieces of wood into clothes pins, or worked on his carvings, one of his favorite pastimes.

Later when Elizabeth decided to take a brief respite from her moving tasks, she went to the window, and while looking outside, savored the little flower garden where she had lovingly nurtured her Sweetbriar, Damask, and Crested Moss roses and then gazed towards the dogwoods and cherry trees, now blossoming in pink perfusion. On countless occasions, after her many tasks were finished, she had basked in their loveliness while working among their sweet scented splendor. When sifting the warm earth through her fingers, it gave her a comforting feeling, which helped sooth her grief after losing Ezra. Somehow, in that little garden, she felt as though her spirit had transcended into a different realm—a place where her soul absorbed its beauty and peace. How she would miss this small haven of hers! Perhaps she could take a few cuttings, she pondered, then concerned about their not surviving her journey, decided that it was best to leave her flowers just as they were, thriving in their native soil. She would have a new home with her beloved Harriet and her family. Everything pertaining to the previous years could be recalled from her treasure chest of memories which she carried within her heart.

The next morning at dawn, Elizabeth once more glanced wistfully at the home she was leaving behind, and while hugging and kissing each of the family members, hoped that her separation from these dear ones, would be brief and that they would visit one another frequently rather than spending many long years apart such as had been the case after Harriet had left New Brunswick Then after making the rounds yet another time, she embraced them all again, and climbed up into buggy with Samuel, her youngest son, who drove her into town to board the stagecoach which would transport her for almost all of her trip, except for the six miles from Aurora to Great Pond. Because the people in that little hamlet utilized that mode of transportation so infrequently when they traveled, the stage coach company didn't find it practical to have a stop there. While boarding the coach, with its cushioned seats and enclosed interior, Elizabeth couldn't help reflecting upon the difference between her present journey and that of Harriet and Simeon ten years previously, during their long, tedious trek through the wilderness in the oxcart. Elizabeth smiled while gazing out the window of the stagecoach, savoring the verdant foliage and some blossoming cherry trees along the roadside. The vestiges of homesickness faded, replaced with a happy expectancy and joy. The beauty of nature had a soothing and transcendent effect on her, just as it did with Harriet, the daughter she would soon embrace after having been apart for so many years.

Most of her journey was uneventful, except for the muddy area which they encountered where the spring rains had saturated the road to the extent that the mud was of such depth as to slow their journey considerably, and the poor horses were mired almost up to their knees. Fortunately, the driver was not only experienced in such conditions, but patient with the hard working animals as well, and encouraged them gently, requesting the passengers to walk alongside for about a mile, until the horses managed to pull the stage through the deepest mud. Another disturbing incident occurred when the passengers were only one mile away from their destination. The driver had suddenly pulled the horses to a stop just in time to avoid colliding with a deer, which was darting across road. When the stagecoach reached the small station in Aurora, though weary from her many hours of travel and feeling cramped in every part of her body, Elizabeth was so filled with thoughts of a joyful reunion with Harriet and her family, that she abruptly experienced a new vigor surging through her being. After the stagecoach driver courteously assisted her down the steep step from the stagecoach, and carried her trunk and cedar chest into the waiting room, she stood at the window while waiting for Harriet and Simeon's horse and wagon to appear to transport her to her new home with them. After a few minutes, a fashionable chaise pulled by a beautiful bay horse stopped outside, and a tall, distinguished looking man stepped out and came into the station. He tipped his hat, smiling, and said, "Are you Mrs. Jennings? I have come to fetch you and to take you to your daughter Harriet's home. Since you two resemble one another so much and because you were the only passenger alighting from the coach, I presumed that you must be her mother."

"Sir, I am," replied Elizabeth, her face filled with concern, "Is Harriet ill? She had planned to meet me here."

"I am sorry that you are alarmed. Harriet is just fine. She was called unexpectedly to deliver a baby, whose mother when into labor early. I am Amos Clark, and my daughter Matilda and Harriet are very close friends. Simeon is caring for the children, and I was very pleased to be able to be of some service to your lovely daughter. She is very dear to me and is responsible for all the happiness that I now enjoy, by reuniting me with my daughter."

"You are very kind to come to provide transportation for the remainder of my journey, Sir," replied Elizabeth. "I hope it does not inconvenience you in any way."

"It certainly does not. I was delighted to have the opportunity to help." Then he gazed at her, smiling, and said, "Please call me Amos, we are to be neighbors and your daughter has welcomed me so warmly into her family circle that I almost feel a part of it, and she and my daughter, Matilda, are almost like sisters."

"Then of course I shall, and you most call me Elizabeth. I am so happy that my Harriet and your daughter are so close. When she left New Brunswick for Great Pond, which at that time was so sparsely populated, still almost a wilderness, I feared that she would be very lonely, and would have few opportunities for friendship."

Sitting there in the comfortable chaise, Elizabeth gazed at the beautiful dogwoods lining the roadside so like the ones back home, and when Amos stopped briefly to allow his horse to rest, she heard birdsong and the soft skittering sounds of small animals among the bushes beside the road. Suddenly she felt at peace with her new surroundings, and the tiny surges of homesickness abated. They traveled about six miles through the tree lined area before she noticed Great Pond's first set of buildings, which consisted of a two story house, well built, with four windows on both the top and bottom floors. The dwelling was painted barn red as was the long shed and the attached barn. She was surprised to see such a modern building in this remote place. As they continued on through the little village, there were other structures, some such as the former one, others unpainted, but all well built and appearing quite comfortable. At the crest of a small hill in the center of the village there was a small white church with a steeple and a two story schoolhouse. Elizabeth was delighted. Harriet had described them in a letter, but she was amazed because they rivaled those of hamlets which had been settled much earlier in New Brunswick. Less than a quarter of a mile ahead, Amos turned into the driveway of her daughter's home, and she was thrilled to see the lovely house, built in the cape style, with its one and a half stories, with a long shed, attached to what looked to be some kind of workshop with perhaps a woodshed below it. The front of the home had two windows on either side of the front door, which had small panes of glass on both sides of it, giving it a decorative appearance. The barn stood several feet away to the right and all the buildings were painted red as was the first structure which she had seen in Great Pond.

Just as Amos took her hand to assist her down the step from the chaise, Harriet, who had only an hour previously successfully delivered a son into the welcoming arms of a neighbor's wife, turned into the driveway, hopped quickly from her wagon, and flew into her mother's arms. When Amos stepped inside his buggy to leave, he turned, gazing at Elizabeth, experiencing feelings he hadn't felt since he had lost Ellen. Then just as he was exiting the driveway, Harriet called him, saying "Papa Amos, please come back and join our celebration of Mama's safe journey to make her home with us."

"But, my dear girl, you haven't seen your mother for so long. I don't wish to intrude."

"You are my adopted Papa now, and are part of our family. You must stay and share our joy!"

"Well, "Daughter", I certainly can never say no to you, so I shall accept your kind invitation." replied Amos, blushing a bit, while thoughts of spending more time with Elizabeth seemed so appealing to him. But shortly after the meal, he noticed Harriet's face, which betrayed her weariness, and said, "It's time I left you two to get some rest, and also I promised Mattie I would come by this evening."

"All right, we shall let you go now and give Mattie my love, but promise that you shall return soon," replied Harriet, giving Amos a hug.

"Of course, My Dear, how could I stay away from my beloved second "daughter" for very long?" said Amos, while leaving somewhat reluctantly.

Elizabeth had also noticed the tiredness, which seemed not only to surge over her daughter's features, but also instead of her customary quick step, she moved slowly, although she made every effort not to display any sign of fatigue. Realizing that Harriet spent hours taking care of her family, and although eleven year old Jennie performed many of the chores, with all the extra work during Simeon's recent illness, as well as her midwife's chores, which sometimes kept her up all night, left little time for sufficient rest to attend to the next day's activities, so she desperately needed her mother's assistance. Elizabeth was grateful that she had made the decision to make her home with her daughter and her family. Also, she arrived the day before Harriet was delivered of her sixth child, Bethiah, and witnessed for the first time the birth of one of her youngest daughter's children. Because of Harriet's extreme weariness, Elizabeth had been concerned that it might affect the birthing. Instead, the baby came so quickly that before Matilda, who had dashed over to deliver the baby the moment Jennie informed her that her mother was in labor, found that all which remained for her to do was to cut the umbilical cord. Relief surged through both mother and dear friend—Matilda's, not only because she was happy because Harriet had been spared suffering, but also, she had worried that should complications arise, her fundamental skills in midwifery might have been inadequate—Elizabeth's, as a mother, along with her prior concern for her daughter's general well being, each stab of pain her child experienced would be as if a knife were penetrating her own heart. Each woman, silently gave a quick prayer of thanks. Then as Matilda, who had her given birth to another hearty son, named for her father, Amos, only a month before, attended to her daughter's needs, Elizabeth gave her granddaughter her first bath. After Harriet had been bathed, had fresh bedding and a clean nightgown, her mother handed her a nice cup of tea, and after she had finished it, placed the infant Bethiah in her arms. While Harriet held the baby, she performed the usual motherly inspection, counting the miniature toes and fingers, and then caressed the soft dark fluff of hair, which already promised to become the exact shade as that of the grandmother whose name she would share.

CHAPTER 19

▼

ANTICIPATION

Not only was Harriet ecstatic about having her mother's companionship after so many years apart, but also felt much more rested with all the assistance she provided by assuming responsibility for much of the work involved in caring and cooking for her large family, as well as cleaning chores, and assisting with the mountains of laundry which accumulated so rapidly in a household with five children. How she had missed Joshua and Bethiah, not only because her love for them had been almost identical to that she felt for her own parents, but because of the many tasks they quietly performed even after they had both become feeble. The countless items of clothing Bethiah had mended, along with watching the children, and making the dough for bread and pies, as well as her advice gleaned from her many years of experience in midwifery and caring for the sick, were only a few of the older women's contributions to the household. Also, Harriet missed Bethiah's affectionate companionship, along with her many other virtues. Joshua had assisted with the making of dozens of candles, mended harnesses, built cradles, and assisted with barn chores. The devoted couple had performed these tasks almost until the end of their earthly lives.

Although Jenny, 11 and Elizabeth, 8, were now able to assist with many of the household chores, as well as assisting Harriet with many other tasks, her work load had remained enormous. After Bethiah's passing, there had never seemed enough hours in the day to accomplish everything which needed to be done. Her mother, though now 56, appeared to be as vigorous and capable as she had been in her youth. Elizabeth's insistence on assuming so many of the household duties greatly alleviated the responsibilities which Harriet had faced without the assistance of Bethiah and Joshua. who, although frail, had assisted in whatever chores they were able to perform.

The dark shadows under Harriet's eyes had disappeared, and the becoming pink was returning to transform her pale face into its former youthful glow. Also, many chores Harriet had performed for Simeon, because of his recent bout with bronchitis had now been taken over by Simeon Jr., 13, and Jamie, 10. He had looked so anguished when his already overtaxed wife performed the barn chores or chopped the wood. Also, Simeon was relieved now that his sons could assume more responsibility in assisting with his own workload, although his feelings were mixed concerning this matter. Now 47, and yet not elderly, he was sensitive about his age because Harriet was sixteen years his junior, and only 31. When Simeon was in his thirties, it didn't appear to matter as much and also, many of his neighbors' wives were much younger than their husbands as well. However, since he had been ill several times recently with bad colds, which in several instances developed into long bouts with bronchitis, along with his prior injuries that placed so many responsibilities upon his wife, had disturbed him a great deal. While pondering the situation, worry lines creased his forehead. As was customary with him when upset about a matter, he ran his fingers through his hair, causing a stray thread of white, which was rapidly spreading through his former raven black hair to fall upon his shoulder. Impatiently, he brushed it off. Then angry with himself for succumbing to negative feelings such as these, he reasoned with himself, realizing that his health had been much less robust, since the several winters he had spent in the woods. When working there the workday had been from daybreak to dusk, and his clothing and boots were constantly either wet or half frozen, as well as having to spending his nights huddled in a common bed with his fellow loggers, in an attempt to keep one another warm under a scanty coverlet, in a cabin with very little heat. In addition to these adverse circumstances, his standing in waist deep water for hours during the logging drives certainly wasn't conducive to retaining good health. Also, he mused, that frigid water must have made me more vulnerable to this touch of rheumatism, which might be causing those pains in my knees, that seem to appear quite often these days. After his recollection of those working conditions, he realized that perhaps his present age was a minor consideration in regard to his health. Of course he would never voice these assumptions to Harriet. It would only cause her to load herself with mountains of guilt, although she realized that he had worked as a logger to provide for not only her, but their children and his parents as well.

Because of the several unusually frigid, lengthy winters delaying the planting of crops, the growing season had been shorter which resulted in scanty harvests. Since the yield of the crops were barely sufficient to feed his family and livestock, there had been nothing to sell for cash needed for to purchase additional food and grain, which left him no alternative, but logging. Also, Harriet would worry that somehow she should have done something more to help, even though the poor girl had exhausted herself performing all that was humanly possible for their welfare herself. His dutiful spouse had worked in Mosbys' store, performed as a midwife, and because of the frail health of Joshua, had performed many of the chores which Simeon would done had he been at home. In addition to all these extra duties, she managed the household frugally and well. In the sparsest of times, she would do what she called "making something out of nothing" by taking a bit of flour and browning it in some saved fat, adding water and whatever seasonings she might have to make a delicious gravy or produce a delicious pudding from a small amount of flour and a few pieces of dried apples. Yes, his petite young wife had performed tasks almost impossible for one of her diminutive size and had done so in some instances during the late stages of a pregnancy when her physical condition was already taxed His thoughts about his work in the logging camps and the log drives possibly having been the cause of his deteriorating health would never be shared with her.

Still in a reflective mood, Simeon wondered, would it have been better to have done as many of our neighbors did—move to Ohio? I certainly was tempted with all its rich farming land and a milder climate as well. Why couldn't I make the decision to leave this place? From the Nathan Jones' glowing reports of Ohio's many advantages, it appears that my family would have found life much easier there. Then suddenly Simeon was aware that he now, despite has feelings when he had left previously to make his home in New Brunswick, now felt the same type of bonding with the land as his father had, and this tiny hamlet, despite its many hardships, was where he was destined to make his home. His work outside in the open fields, and within the dense forests, savoring the pure air scented by nature's wildflowers, the delicate perfume of fresh cut grass, and the tangy fragrance of the pines, spruces, cedars, and hemlocks within the quiet, secluded places, provided him with a sense of freedom he had never enjoyed while working inside the confining walls of his cobbler shop. Finally he understood, at least partially, why Joshua had left a thriving business, his Grist Mill, which provided his family with a comfortable home and prosperous life style, to settle what was at the time he arrived, a dense wilderness. Also, he was very relieved because Harriet appeared to share his feelings, and now that her mother shared the responsibilities of the family, providing her with so much assistance, she actually had some time for leisure. How thankful he was that this vigorous, loving woman had come to make her home with them.

Simeon glanced with satisfaction at the house he had recently renovated. How thankful he was that his work on the open chamber was completed before his mother-in-law's arrival. Its open space had been converted into two additional bedrooms, which provided one for her, and another for his three daughters, who were delighted with their spacious new bedroom, so much larger than the cramped area which they shared previously. Also, Simeon felt that the decision he and his father had made to build the house with its one and one half stories and pitched roof in the style people referred to as a Cape, was wise. Although the bedrooms had only partially flat ceilings sloping on one side, they were high enough to afford comfortable space. Also, the area between the walls and the eaves left room for built in drawers as well as a portion to provide both storage space and a delightful little place for the children to play, perhaps pretending that they were in a secret room, cave or whatever else they might fancy. Simeon smiled when accessing his workmanship on the home he had provided for his family, and while answering Harriet's call to come in for supper, his step was lighter—the prior weariness seemed to fall away as though he were shedding a 100 pound sack of cement from his shoulders. Impulsively, he walked over to the pasture gate, climbed upon it just as one of his children might have done, gazed over the fields below to the place where the forest bordered the pasture, and noticed two deer in their summer camouflage of orange tan, frolicking over the verdant grass. Simeon felt a surge of kinship with this beautiful vista, and mused that had he been born a king, he couldn't have possessed a greater domain.

CHAPTER 20

▼

THE STORM

The storm invaded the peaceful evening with terrifying intensity, following the mildest weather Simeon could ever remember experiencing in January. Icy chunks of hail pummeled against the roof, and the front door which hadn't been closed tightly, flew open. The tumultuous force of the winds almost threw Simeon to the floor as he attempted to close it. He managed to do so after bracing himself against a heavy hall table, but not before several shards of frozen rain littered the floor. Simeon's face was clouded with concern for the possible damage to the house, outbuildings, and barn, so he quickly threw on his heavy wool jacket, and dashed outside to close and secure the blinds which would assist in protecting the windows from the onslaught of the storm. He then proceeded to the woodshed to bring in extra wood. As the storm progressed, the house cooled off considerably, despite its snug windows and the banking of tarred paper, which was covered with evergreen branches. Simeon placed an additional log atop the waning blaze in the fireplace and stoked up the kitchen range, adding some good hardwood pieces which would provide a nice steady warmth. Outside, the fury of the storm accelerated, and the furious howling of the wind resembled that of some angry monster on a rampage.

Just as Harriet entered the room with steaming mugs of hot chocolate, Simeon's fears concerning the safety of his family's property during the storm were realized. The heavy winds had torn several shingles from the roof, and when he anxiously peered through the little window panes lining the sides of the front door, their broken pieces were blowing across the snow covered lawn, swept along by the wind's icy blasts as effortlessly as though they were bits of confetti. The storm was celebrating its victory over the puny efforts of man to control its plundering. Simeon again donned his soaked wool jacket, hurried to the shed to get his ladder, a large piece of canvas, and some nails to fasten against the roof to cover the area where the shingles had been ripped off by the gale force winds. By the time he began to climb the ladder in order to perform the repairs, Harriet, who had been comforting the startled baby, awakened from his nap by the storm, followed Simeon, and clutching his arm, pleaded, "Simeon, please don't attempt to climb up upon the roof. Not only will the ladder be in danger of being shaken by the wind, but the entire top of the house must be covered with sleet. It is just too dangerous!"

Simeon pulled away from her, replying, "Harriet, this icy mess will be coming through the ceilings any moment now and everything will be soaked. Not to mention all my hard work in renovating those rooms. I must go."

Simmy rushed in and said, "Dad, I will come too. I can hold the ladder while you are climbing up to the roof and then I can come up to help you."

"Thank you, Son. You may hold the ladder but I forbid you to come up on the roof. It's too hazardous."

"It is too precarious a job for either one of you during this terrible storm," Harriet said, her face etched with concern. "Even if the ceilings are damaged, it would be much worse if you are injured! Please, I beg you, Simeon, wait until the winds have subsided and this terrible freezing rain has stopped!"

Elizabeth interceded, saying, "My dear Simeon, I do not usually condone a mother-in-law's meddling, but in this case, I feel I must also voice my concerns. I agree with Harriet. This ice storm is much too unsafe for anyone to venture outside, let alone climbing about on a roof."

Disregarding their pleas, Simeon ascended the ladder while Simmy put all his weight against it to prevent it from sliding, until his father had placed his feet atop the sloping roof. Instead of returning to the warmth of the house, he remained outside in the event that his dad might lose his footing or some other type of mishap should occur. In Simmy's haste to assist him, he had neglected to button his coat, which was already sodden, as well as his woolen shirt underneath, because the strength of the wind had driven the icy rain against his unprotected chest. Nevertheless, he stood there in his half frozen garments, with his teeth chattering from the cold, and waited while Simeon was performing his task in order to be there in the event an accident occurred. After ten minutes elapsed, Harriet donned her coat, ran outside, and pulled her unwilling son inside to change into the warm, dry clothing, which Elizabeth had assembled for him. Aferwards, she insisted that he sit beside fireplace to assist in warming his shivering body, and presented him with a steaming cup of hot chocolate. When Simmy had been made comfortable, despite her mother's protests, Harriet assumed her son's vigil beside the ladder. Icy pellets stung her face and within moments her clothing felt as though it were a slab of ice. And what of Simeon, she agonized, while watching her husband fearfully. He had been exposed to the storm's fury for at least thirty minutes. Stubbornly, he just kept pounding in nails to secure the canvas, amid her pleas for him to come down. After having been exposed to the bitter cold for so long, his clothing must be frozen to his body, Harriet despaired Her own hands already ached because of the frigid temperature. How could he continue to work with his after having been exposed to the storm for such a length of time? She wondered. Despite the menacing blasts of wind, Simeon managed to secure the canvas which provided a temporary patch to the damaged area of the roof that was at least five feet in diameter Just as he stepped back to survey his patching job, while Harriet watched helplessly, his foot slipped, and he plummeted off the roof, landing in a pile of snow which was about five feet high. Although it broke his fall somewhat, the mound was deeply frozen and permeated with fallen icicles protruding from the icy mass.

Harriet screamed while racing towards him. Despite the clamor of the wind, Elizabeth heard her terrified cries for assistance, and immediately, She along with Simmy, and Jamie, dashed outside to assist in carrying Simeon, who was now unconscious, into the house After placing him on the daybed in the kitchen, Harriet bent down to listen for his heartbeat and after a few intensely stressful moments, was tremendously relieved to hear a faint, but steady beat and his breathing, although labored, was audible. Carefully, Harriet removed his icy garments, and she and her mother gently examined his body for injuries. A large bump was already forming on the back of his head, and he appeared to have several broken ribs, but fortunately, neither his arms nor legs appeared to be broken. They applied an arnica poultice to the protrusion on his head, and then dipped soft linen clothes into a solution composed of a mixture of arnica tincture and water to soothe the area of his body where his ribs had been broken. After several applications had dried, they wound thick strips of tapes around his chest to protect and assist the healing of his ribs. After this, Simeon's eyes fluttered open, and he complained of a splitting headache. Elizabeth held a cup of steaming chamomile tea to his lips, which after a few minutes, helped sooth his pain somewhat. Both Harriet and her mother determined that Simeon's unconscious state was caused by striking his head against one of the hard particles of the protruding icicles and that this had caused a mild concussion. "What a relief! It could have been so much worse," Harriet said and then added "Thank you, Dear Lord." While the two women had attended to Simeon's injuries, Harriet's thoughts flashed back to that summer's day several years ago, remembering his previous injury which had occurred when he had been hurt when being dragged by a horse several years before, and at that time Bethiah was there to assist and comfort her. How grateful Harriet felt that her mother had come to make her home with them and she was extremely grateful for her presence.

The next day Jonathan, Amy, Little Ben, and Baby Susan, came to visit, not only because they usually did so regularly, but also they had been concerned about the family's safety during the storm. After learning about Simeon's injury, Jonathan insisted upon repairing the damaged roof, even though Simeon, who was shaky and sore from his injuries, protested stubbornly that he would attend to the job himself. Finally after a brief period of resistance, he agreed to Jonathan's performing the task. Harriet sighed deeply with relief, and was thankful that her cousin had come to her assistance as he had done when Simeon had been injured previously, on that summer's day several years before, when an impending thunder storm was threatening to ruin the freshly cut hay. He had not only assisted her in harvesting the fodder before the downpour began, but he remained with them as well, taking over many of Simeon's tasks while his injuries were healing. Jonathan had also been of tremendous help when he set Simeon's leg, which had been fractured during an incident with a horse. The animal, frightened by a loud thunderclap, had dragged him through a rocky field. Jonathan's strong hands had been invaluable in the setting of the injured limb, as was his knowledge of Indian medicine, which had been gleaned during his ten years spent with them. He had taken supple but sturdy strips of bark, securing them with leather thongs in order to fashion a cast for the broken limb. How wonderful it was to have caring, loving people around her, always happy to assist in any way in which they might be needed, Harriet mused. Also, Simmy, at this point, could assume many of the tasks Simeon usually performed. In addition to her son's assistance, her oldest daughter, Jennie was performing many of the household tasks, as well as learning to make delicious pies, cakes and preparing delicious meals. Her molasses cookies were beginning to taste almost like her grandmother's. Only a day after she arrived from New Brunswick Elizabeth had baked some of those delicious morsels, which were Harriet's favorite sweet. She had been outside working in her flower garden when she savored their delightful aroma which flitted through the open kitchen window, and just as she had as a child, ran inside to enjoy one, warm from the long, rectangular cookie sheet.

Then she munched on it as eagerly as she had so many years before, and for those fleeting moments, she retreated into the world of the little girl she had been. They were large rounds almost cake-like in consistency, with their tops criss-crossed with a fork and sprinkled with sugar, and somehow her mother managed to add just the exact amount of each spice, cinnamon, nutmeg, and a touch of cloves to make them equally delectable every time. Although Harriet 's own baking won many compliments, her molasses cookies, no matter how much she attempted to duplicate her mother's, never quite tasted the same. Yes, she mused, it is so wonderful to have Mama here, and I am also grateful for all the responsibilities which have been lifted from my shoulders, by mother and my older children. Then quite unexpectedly, a stray thought flickered through her psyche, as sometimes happens, even though having nothing to do with the present circumstances, causing her to wonder if the muse might, after such a long absence, revisit her with inspiration for a poem or a painting.

CHAPTER 21

▼

DILEMMA

Although Elizabeth occasionally felt surges of homesickness for the family and the home she had left in New Brunswick, during the first few weeks after her arrival in the tiny village of Great Pond, she was delighted to be with Harriet and Simeon as well as the grandchildren she was acquainting herself with for the first time. Also, the small hamlet was expanding slowly, but steadily, with five more families arriving during the past year to make their homes there. Summer breezes drifted through the kitchen window, and the scent of the abundant wild roses which covered their verdant bushes in pink profusion, had delighted Harriet when she had first come to live there, and now these lovely flowers were a source of joy to her mother as well Elizabeth stood at the window for a moment, breathing in their fragrant perfume. Then glancing at the clock, she was suddenly aware that the large mound of bread dough she had finished kneading prior to her short respite from her chores, must be put to rise immediately in order for it to be ready to bake for supper. Quickly, she placed it in a large bowl and covered it with a red checked dishtowel to rise. Since the kitchen would be heated from the baking Elizabeth had planned for the afternoon, its warmth would accelerate the rising of the dough, and there would be sufficient time for it to double in size, be punched down, replaced in the bowl once more to climb to the top of the dish, then shaped into loaves, and after rising for a brief time, placed in the oven to be baked for the evening meal. Harriet had invited Amos Clark to have supper with them and Elizabeth would make not only the bread, but her special strawberry rhubarb pie with its golden brown, flaky crust. She brushed the crust with a little beaten egg yolk, which never failed to give the pie an evenly browned, nicely glazed appearance. I hope this turns out well, she mused, and suddenly wondered why she was so concerned with her baking. After having produced hundreds of pies throughout the years, why am I worried over the perfection of this one? Elizabeth wondered. Suddenly, almost unconsciously, she blushed such as a teen aged girl might have done, while anticipating her first date with a young man. Well, of course, every woman wishes to have good results with her baking, she reasoned. Although she didn't wish to admit it, even to herself, Elizabeth was aware it was important to her that her pie was especially delicious, because she hoped that Amos would enjoy it. What is the matter with me, she whispered to herself. I want the meals he shares with us, as well as everything else in our relationship to be perfect, and yet I keep refusing to put myself in a position to be alone with him. I am behaving as if I were a young woman who doesn't know how she feels about a possible suitor. We are both well past middle age. Why am I so confused about my feelings for him? When he asked me to accompany him on a drive after supper tonight, what made me cause him to wait for my answer by telling him I will let him know after the meal? How silly I am to be so indecisive and nervous about it, Elizabeth mused.

While she ground the coffee, and dipped water from the pail on the counter to fill the pot, putting it towards to rear of the stove to perk slowly so it wouldn't be too strong, but ready when the dessert was served, her thoughts again returned to Amos. Finally she admitted to herself why she was so hesitant to accept his invitations involving her company. I really do know what the problem is—I am afraid he will propose and I don't know how to handle the situation. Usually all this soul searching would have been shared with Harriet, but somehow, Elizabeth couldn't bring herself to expose these particular concerns with anyone, even her beloved daughter. She laid the table, using the silver she had brought with her from New Brunswick, as well as Harriet's new set of china. After completing all her tasks involving the meal, she sighed deeply murmuring to herself, "I really do care for Amos. In fact I think I love him, but can I be a wife again? After losing Ezra, it took me so long to put my life back together again. Can I risk possibly outliving another husband?" Then she recalled the trauma of loneliness, and the many nights after her husband's passing, when she had reached over towards his side of the bed with a caressing touch and her hand had felt only emptiness. Agonizing further, she remembered all the holidays and anniversaries when after having felt that finally she was beginning to cope with her grief, it would return, surging through her being like an unpredictable storm. Several years later, she became aware that those family occasions, now incomplete without Ezra, were the reason she had returned to her mire of despair Elizabeth's eyes filled with tears, and she wondered what had happened to the stoic person she had been previously. Resolutely, she forced her thoughts away from the past. While placing the pie in the oven, her thoughts drifted to the occasion when Amos had arrived at the stagecoach station to provide her with transportation for the six mile distance to Harriet and Simeon's home. When they met, the feelings that she had been certain would lie forever dormant within her, were suddenly revived. Although Elizabeth had long since dropped all vestiges of girlish shyness when around the opposite sex, she had felt as if she were a young maiden again, and her face had turned crimson, when he had taken her hand to assist her while she descended the steep steps of the stage. Also, she had blushed again while stealing a glance at his handsome face, because at the same moment he turned to gaze at hers. Then his face colored as well. They both felt it, she was certain. She sensed it in the expression in his eyes when he assisted her into his chaise. Love at first sight? How could it be at our ages, she mused, smiling. Then she brushed the tops of the biscuits with butter before popping them into the oven, so they would turn golden brown as they baked, and once again her thoughts turned to yet another reason why it might not be wise to accept a marriage proposal at this time. What of the assistance she was providing to Harriet, one of the motivating forces which had impelled her to leave New Brunswick and come to make her home with her daughter and son-in-law? I have been here for only two years at this point, and it would be just as though I were dashing away and leaving her with all her chores and childcare to attend to without the assistance I had planned to give her for whatever length of time she needs it. Then, momentarily, she glanced outside the kitchen window, and noticed a darting hummingbird, flitting back and forth among the day lilies, swooping to sip nectar from their succulent vials, and after its repast, flew away so rapidly, that the little bird became only a miniscule speck in the distance within seconds. Elizabeth stepped back from the window, took the perfectly raised and browned biscuits from the oven and set them on the counter to cool just a moment before she placed them in a cloth lined basket to keep them warm while readying the remainder of the meal for serving. Again, she smiled, while contemplating the hummingbird, and murmured aloud to herself, "Life is much like that tiny creature's flight. It speeds on so quickly that sometimes we are not aware of its passing, let alone how quickly children become adults or how quickly they can assume so many helpful tasks. It does not seem possible that Jennie is almost thirteen now, and Elizabeth is ten. Both girls are already of great assistance to Harriet and Simmy is fifteen, Jamie, is twelve, Joshua eight, and little Bethiah is two. It seems almost unbelievable that it is 1833, and that my grandchildren are growing up so quickly.

"Yes, she mused, Harriet doesn't need my assistance as much as she did previously, and life is rushing by almost as rapidly as the flight of that little hummingbird. We must all savor every moment of it.

Amos would be arriving any minute. Again her thoughts turned to him realizing that she must give him an answer not only whether or not she would accept his invitation for a drive, but in the event he proposed marriage, decide what her answer would be. And again sighing deeply, she wondered, perhaps I am only imagining that he might do so. Perhaps he is afraid of losing another wife, just as I have been fearful that if remarrying, I might possibly outlive another husband. Amos's loss of his Ellen had traumatized him to the point that he had not only become cold and indifferent to the world, but also had treated his daughter so unfairly. One evening when they had sat together alone for a few minutes, while the children were in bed, and Harriet and Simeon were busy in the barn with a heifer, who was having difficulties calving, he had told her, with tears of remorse welling up in his eyes, about the years of neglect and mistreatment of his only child. Also, Amos had said that he would be eternally grateful to Harriet, who had helped him return to the kind, loving man he had been before he went into his cold, bleak shell after the loss of his wife. After his confession, Elizabeth found it difficult to believe that this gentle, affectionate man sitting there beside her, who was so devoted to his daughter, his grandsons, Albert and his namesake little Amos, as well as his son-in-law whom he had previously disapproved, had ever been in a state such as this. Momentarily, she had been angry with him for his past. That is, until she saw the agony in his face. She then reached over gently, patting his shoulder, with the same forgiving, caring gesture as Harriet had displayed when accompanying him in his chaise during his trip to Great Pond to reconcile with his daughter and beg for her forgiveness. After observing his tears of remorse, she had reached into his pocket, taken his handkerchief, and wiped away his tears of remorse. Suddenly Elizabeth smiled, took off her apron, and when she gazed out the kitchen window and saw him approaching, her step was light as a young girl's as she hurried to the door to welcome him.

CHAPTER 22

▼

DECISION

After the supper, which had resulted in several compliments from Amos for Elizabeth's delicious strawberry rhubarb pie and light, fluffy biscuits, as well as Harriet's tasty pot roast, Jennie, Elizabeth and Harriet cleared the table and headed for the pantry to wash the dishes. Amos and Simeon each took one of the varnished wooden rocking chairs to chat until the women would return to join the conversation after the remainder of the food was put away and the dish washing was finished. Almost immediately after the men were seated, Simeon noticed that his guest appeared to be restless and instead of his usual lively input to the conversation, was quiet and meditative. Simeon hesitated for a few moments and then asked, "Is something bothering you, Amos? You do not seem quite yourself tonight."

Amos smiled while replying, "I'm sorry. Nothing is wrong. I didn't realize that my face was betraying my concern regarding how your mother-in-law will respond to the question I shall ask her when she joins me later this evening for a ride in my chaise."

"My dear Amos, now you really have aroused my curiosity. What secret have you been keeping from me? Your face is turning rather crimson. Is it possible that a romance is budding between you and Mother Elizabeth?"

"Yes, my good friend. It has gone far beyond the budding stage. I have loved her ever since the first day I met her when I picked her up in my carriage at the stage station to bring her here. Tonight I plan to ask her to be my wife. Do I have your blessing?" And what do you suppose that Harriet's feelings will be if her mother and I marry? After all that dear girl has done for me, the last thing I would ever do is something which might cause her any distress."

"Amos," Simeon said, smiling, "Of course you have my blessing and I'm sure you have Harriet's as well. You know she has loved you as a father for some time. Also, your revelation is not as secret as you may have believed. Harriet and I have observed the manner in which you and Mother Elizabeth behave when you are together. You both blush when your hands touch one another's. Also, you each have eyes that express what your words do not. We have been expecting you to declare your affection, one of these days."

"Do you think she will have me?"

"Yes, I most certainly do, but she is coming through the door right now, so you two be off, and end this suspense."

While Amos took Elizabeth's hand to assist her into the buggy, he felt as awkward as he had at twenty, and blushed deeply. Elizabeth's face was also crimson and then she smiled unexpectedly. Why are the two of us are acting like shy young lovers, not as one who is 56 and the other 58? But isn't love always the same, she pondered. Then after meditating momentarily, she realized that it was.

Amos, noticing her affectionate smile, gained the courage to blurt out, despite his careful rehearsal to himself of his proposal, "My darling, will you marry me? I have loved you since the moment I saw you!"

Elizabeth gazed into his eyes, filled with love, and simply said, "Yes, Amos, my dear, I will. I have loved you, since I first saw you as well, although many times I didn't want to admit it to myself. You see, I was so afraid of taking a chance on the possibility of outliving another husband."

"Oh my dearest," he said, shyly caressing her, "I understand. I also felt that way at first, because of losing Ellen. But we will savor whatever time we have together, whether it be many years or few."

Although both Harriet and Matilda were both ecstatic about the upcoming marriage of Amos and Elizabeth, and attempted to plan a wedding for them, complete with a reception which would include all their neighbors, they lovingly declined the offer. Two weeks later, the couple quietly left a note for each daughter, took the stage coach to Bangor and eloped. As a surprise for his beloved bride, Amos had arranged passage there for a steamship which would transport them to Boston where the couple would honeymoon for two weeks. Both astounded and delighted, Elizabeth threw her arms around her new husband, saying, "I am completely overwhelmed, my love. Never in my wildest dreams did I ever hope to go to Boston, let alone remain there for two whole weeks! It must be tremendously expensive. And this hotel! What sumptuous meals and accommodations! You need not spoil me you know. I am accustomed to only simple pleasures."

"My Darling wife," replied Amos, "I am a wealthy man and can well afford to pamper my bride with a few presents. Finally, after all these empty years, I have you to share my life with. Please humor me, My Dear. It gives me great pleasure to provide some luxuries for you." "And," He said, smiling, "There's more to come."

Before Elizabeth could reply, she heard a tapping on the door, which Amos opened to admit a young man whose arms were filled with beautifully decorated boxes. Then he brought in several others that were heaped upon the floor beside the room's entrance, placing them all upon a large, highly polished table beside the chair in which Elizabeth was sitting.

"Oh Amos, what is all this?" she asked.

"Just a few presents for my bride!"

"My dear husband, what have you done? Bought out several stores? You already gave me such a beautiful ruby and diamond wedding ring." Then Elizabeth leaned against the high backed velvet covered, deeply cushioned chair, with the excitement of a child opening Christmas presents. Each beribboned box held its own treasure. The first one which she unwrapped displayed a black velvet box and inside sat a ring whose center held a sparkling blue sapphire encircled with two diamonds on either side of its setting. Another similar box contained an emerald necklace with earrings to match. Inside the other packages were three shimmering silk dresses, one deep blue, one such a deep rose color, it was almost crimson, and the other as yellow as her favorite roses which had bloomed in her New Brunswick garden. Yet another parcel contained a street length velvet cape, and the oblong boxes held three pairs of satin slippers, which matched each of the three dresses, as well as a comfortable pair of boots, suitable for walking.

Almost too overwhelmed to speak, she threw her arms around her new husband, and murmured, "Amos, my darling, a thousand thanks for all these lovely gifts, but you should not have given me so many. These lovely things must have cost a fortune!" Then she added, "And, by the way, my love, how did you know my dress and boot sizes?"

"I employed the assistance of your dear daughter, my lovely wife. She provided me with your measurements and shoe sizes." "And," he added, "Please just give me the pleasure of indulging you, My Dearest. It gives me much pleasure."

"Oh, I am sorry! I didn't intend to appear unappreciative! I'm so overwhelmed and not accustomed to such luxury. Then she rather shyly put her arms around his neck and caressed him. He returned her kisses and they stood there enclosed in one another's arms, each experiencing the loneliness of so many years melting away almost as rapidly as when the caress of the spring sun causes the winter weary earth to shed its snow-covered garments to don the vibrant blossoms of spring.

Later that night, lying there beside her sleeping husband, Elizabeth lay quietly, not wishing to disturb him while sleep eluded her, despite all the traveling and activity. Suddenly, she realized why. It was the old guilt that engulfed her from time to time—the old gnawing question, why was Ezra taken instead of her? And here she was surrounded by such indulgence, when he had worked so hard for a modest livelihood and had not lived long enough to enjoy the leisure of advancing age? Then suddenly, she reasoned with herself, that Ezra was with God, living within heavenly realms. Quite unexpectedly, she felt her whole being emanating with a profound peace and she smiled, gazing lovingly at her bridegroom, basking in her new found happiness.

CHAPTER 23

▼

CONCERNS

Harriet stood by the kitchen window, then opened it and immediately the scent of lilacs filled the room with their fragrance. Each year, their lovely purple blooms provided spring bouquets for a lovely adornment to the rooms, celebrating the end of the cold months of winter. But yet, the time has flown though, she mused. It seems as if such a short time has elapsed since we were banking the house against the winter cold and now it is nearly time for lighter bedding and spring cleaning! I can hardly believe that it is 1838! While she gathered a bouquet of lilacs, her thoughts drifted to Simmy, who was now twenty, and would marry Lucinda Hampton, a neighbor's daughter in less than a month. It seems as though he was just a little boy just a few years ago. Her face glowing with happiness for her oldest son, she mused about the lovely girl he had chosen to be his bride. Lucinda had accepted his proposal promptly without displaying the coyness of some of the pretty girls who had basked in the attentions of many suitors, although she also, had more than her share of young men seeking her hand in marriage. The young couple would move into the large bedroom which Elizabeth had used during her stay with the family. Harriet sighed contentedly, grateful that her son and his bride would be content to live in his family home. Not that she would have attempted to deter them from living elsewhere, but was relieved when they had made their decision to remain in the Wilson home place, at least for the time being. Simeon's health had deteriorated in the past few years. Her face clouded with sadness, when wondering if his work in the lumber camps during those difficult winters when they were so short of money, might have made him more susceptible to the rheumatism which was now causing him so much discomfort Was there anything more she could have done to assist Simeon, so he wouldn't have felt obligated to earn the much needed funds in this manner? Then reviewing those hardscrabble times, Harriet realized that she had been as frugal as possible and had contributed as much toward to the family's sustenance as she could have. Also, she feared, because he was sixteen years her senior, quite possibly she would outlive him. The very thought of life without her dear husband was devastating and she forced herself to concentrate on her son's approaching wedding.

However, despite Harriet's attempts to dwell upon happy events, her troubling thoughts shifted to Jennie, who was also planning to wed. In two months, she would wed Nathan Collins son, Ethan, whom both Harriet and Simeon were fond of. He was a kind and considerate young man, who at thirty, was twelve years older than Jennie, and had become a widower when his wife, Emma, had been assumed to have drowned during the sinking of a steamboat during a violent storm which occurred when she had been aboard the vessel traveling to visit her family in Boston. After seven years had passed and although some of the passengers had not been accounted for, she was assumed to have lost her life, along with most of the other passengers. The only apparent survivors were the two young men who had managed to cling to a portion of the ship's flooring until a fishing boat appeared and rescued them. Because it was during the haying season, Ethan had remained at home to assist with this vital task. The grief stricken young husband had not only mourned his lost wife, but blamed himself as well, believing perhaps, if he, a strong swimmer, had been there, it might have been possible for him to have saved her life. Then after so much time had elapsed that Ethan had lost all hope of learning what her fate had been, he received a letter from the steamship company informing him that one of the survivors had attempted to rescue someone fitting Emma's description, but because of the intensity of the storm and churning water, she was snatched away from his grip and drowned. Wondering why such a long span of time had elapsed before the survivor came forward with the information about his lost wife, he contacted the company, which replied that the person had been in such a state of shock from his experience, that it had just occurred to him that the information about his rescue attempt would be helpful in determining what had happened to the young woman during the sinking of the ship. Finally Ethan realized that he must go on with his life, and began courting Jennie and soon fell in love with the cheerful, pretty young woman. Certainly because he was a widower and twelve years her senior, was not a matter of concern for Harriet, and also, she did not consider her oldest daughter too young for marriage—she had been only sixteen when marrying Simeon. What caused her despair, was that the couple, immediately after their wedding, would leave for Ohio. Jennie and Ethan, just as many other New Englanders had done, who had already left New England for the many advantages this part of the country offered, planned to make this State their home. So far away, she agonized, and although I knew how sad Mama was when I left my family in New Brunswick with Simeon to assist his aging parents who needed us so badly, my feelings about Jenny's move, emphasizes even more how difficult it must have been for her. Despite this, she didn't attempt to discourage us from leaving, not only because she knew that Simeon's parents desperately required our help, but also, I guess she handled the situation in a much wiser and understanding manner than I am this one, even though I was the first of her children to leave home. Perhaps to alleviate her self criticism, she rationalized that this was a different situation. She had not desired to leave nor did Simeon, but both had felt that they had no other choice, conscience wise, and Jennie seems just as eager as Ethan does, to make their home in Ohio, with all its fertile land, and so many opportunities. Continuing her reverie despite desperately attempting not to do so, she sighed and murmured to herself, Oh dear, what is wrong with me, I used to be almost as stoic as Mama is, and I must enjoy this lovely day the Lord has made and dwell upon happy thoughts. My children are growing up to be kind and hard working people and have their own lives and possess the wisdom for the choices they must make. Mama is so happy with Papa Amos and so many marvelous events are taking place in Ohio and many other states in this young country of ours as well. A steam ship has already crossed the Atlantic Ocean without using sails to augment its engine which had been the case when the voyage was attempted in 1819. Stagecoaches make traveling so much easier and have routes that provide connections for transportation by steamships and railroads, which are spreading all over the place, speeding along on those tracks. Making a journey is so much faster and more comfortable! Perhaps some day I can go to visit Jennie or she can come to visit us with all those new modes of transit. Harriet contented herself with this thought and busied herself with making a nice gingerbread for supper. It would be served with lots of rich whipped cream and was a family favorite. Yawning, she leaned against the counter wearily while grating a piece of ginger root. It had been a long, tedious, night and the birthing she had attended to, had been so difficult that at one point, Harriet had been fearful that both mother and child would be lost. Thankfully, both survived, and Harriet again breathed a prayer of gratitude.

After finishing her baking, she took out the lovely ivory silk material which was a gift from Matilda to be utilized in the making of Jenny's wedding dress. Sitting by the window with the afternoon sun illuminating the room was an ideal time to sew, because it provided much more light than when depending on candles for illumination. For a few minutes Harriet worked peacefully, feeling the tranquility she had always felt when doing something creative. Then suddenly, after pricking her finger with the needle, and quickly snatching her handkerchief and wrapping her finger with it to prevent staining the material, she suddenly began sobbing. It was as though she had pierced her heart instead of sustaining a tiny wound on her finger. Despite her resolute intentions to avoid dwelling upon Jenny's forthcoming move, she had allowed herself to do so, succumbing to her emotions, as many people do when overtired, because this state causes them to be so much more susceptible. Handling fabric which would become Jenny's wedding dress was not a task that she should be attempting today, Harriet mused. What happened to me? I have always tried to show courage and faith when sad challenges must be faced. I must concentrate on something else for now, she sighed, and feeling totally disgusted with herself, she returned the half stitched garment to its box.

After Harriet drank a soothing cup of tea and tidied the kitchen, her thoughts drifted to her mother's marriage. Mama and Papa Amos have been married for five years now! She smiled, while brushing away a strand of hair, noticing that it's red gold hues, were now touched with a little gray. He treats her like a queen, and is not only such a wonderful husband for her, but also a loving step father and grandfather as well. What a transformation from that day so long ago where I invaded his office because of his harsh treatment of his daughter. How close they are now! And he adores his grandsons. No one could believe that he had ever been the man he was then. But of course, she mused, he wasn't really that man. Now he is the person he really was before the loss of his wife. Immediately after his reconciliation with Matilda, because of his desire to live near his daughter and grandson., Amos had sold his lumber mill and his ornate house in Bangor. After moving to Great Pond he built another house, quite modest in comparison, within walking distance of their home. Harriet, smiled, feeling a little less sad, and after picking some sweet green peas which had grown just enough to be nice and tender, decided to sit on the wooden bench beside her flower garden while she shelled them for supper. When popping the tiny peas from their pods, she suddenly remembered that as child she had so much fun using seed cases from peas such as these for tiny "canoes," which she fashioned by placing a tiny strip of wood in their centers . Where have those years gone? She pondered. I am a grandmother now! That happy little reminiscence and the scent of the apple blossoms permeating the air, along with the warm spring breezes tousling her hair, momentarily transported her into that peaceful little world she had savored so many years ago when she was a little girl in New Brunswick. Her step was lighter and some of the weariness she had experienced throughout the day, because of her spending must of the night delivering a baby, slipped away while she returned to the kitchen to prepare the evening meal.

CHAPTER 24

▼

JENNIE

The day was breathtakingly beautiful, with balmy breezes, and benevolent touches of the spring sun caressed the faces of the flowers in Elizabeth's garden. While gazing through the parlor window observing their loveliness, she found the scene so irresistible that she ventured outside with the exuberance of a young girl to savor its beauty. While Elizabeth sat in the comfortable wooden chair, whose seat had been padded by Amos to add to her comfort, she not only enjoyed its present abundant flowering, but basked in anticipation when observing the emerging of the roses' tiny buds. In just a few weeks the garden would be transformed into glorious blooms of various shades of crimson, deep pink, yellow, and white, and the lovely little pond beside the garden, complete with water lilies, whose delicate perfumed flowers would soon open to flow languidly in the clear, cool, water. This beautiful little haven was only one of the many surprises Amos had ready for her when she arrived to make her home with him as his bride. Then as if that wasn't enough, two months later, he added a lovely veranda as well as two additional rooms to the house, despite her protests that it was spacious enough just as it was. "But, my dear," Amos replied, "Now there will be plenty of room for your family members in New Brunswick when they come to visit us."

After having been married to Amos for the past five years, Elizabeth was finally learning to accept his caring indulgences without protesting quite as much as she had previously At this point, when he presented her with one of his frequent gifts or surprises, instead of further ado, she just reached up, put her arms around him, murmured her thanks, and kissed him. Life with Amos provided her with more happiness than she ever dreamed was possible, and she was constantly amazed because their ages didn't appear to have any significance at all. Their love, although a mature one, made marriage as exciting and exuberant as if they were both in their twenties, instead of their early sixties, and this revelation caused her to realize that true love is as ageless as the recurrence of the verdant foliage of trees and the lush blooming of the wild roses and lilacs each spring. Also, Amos's dear Mattie, had welcomed her into the family warmly and regarded her as a mother figure from the moment she learned of their coming marriage. How grateful she was for that! Just at that moment, Matilda appeared at the garden gate, saying, Mother Elizabeth, little Amos and I are going over to visit Harriet for a while. Would you and Papa like to come with us?"

"I would love to, my dear. Your papa is gathering some lilacs for a bouquet. Let us go out and surprise him." Then she kissed Matilda's cheek, giving her a hug, and bent down to caress her little step grandson, saying, "My goodness, Amos, .it seems as though you are growing taller every day!."

"Yes, I am a big boy now and soon I shall be helping Papa in the store just like my brother Albert is doing right now!" he replied.

"I am sure you shall," Elizabeth murmured, while giving him a kiss on his rosy little cheek. Each time she saw the child, his resemblance to his grandfather appeared more pronounced. Elizabeth took the sturdy little five year olds hand, and together they found Amos coming towards them with his lovely bouquet of fragrant purple blooms from the lilac bushes, which he loved to pick for Elizabeth, because she so loved their scent in the house. His little namesake dashed towards him calling, "Grandpa! Grandpa! We have come to take you to visit Aunt Harriet with us!"

Then he ran over to hug his six foot tall grandfather, and although the child's height was above average for a five year old, his arms barely reached Amos's knees. With his face radiant with love, he bent down and swooping the small boy into his arms, gave him a big hug, and placed him astride his shoulders for the piggyback ride the child always loved. This man, who had isolated himself from everyone precious to him for so many years, wondered at times whether he deserved the tremendously blissful life he had experienced, since Harriet's visit that day eleven years ago. After he was newly reconciled with his daughter he didn't believe that he could have been happier, but when she bore his grandsons, without losing her life as her mother had, his life was ever more joyous. And now, his marriage to his adored Elizabeth, made him even more ecstatic and richly blessed.

His happy reverie, was interrupted when his grandson asked, "Grandpa, can we just walk over the Aunt Harriet's, instead of taking your chaise?"

"But I thought you loved to ride in the chaise," Amos replied.

"If we do, you can't give me a piggy back ride all the way like you could if we walked."

"Darling boy, what if your mother and grandmother Elizabeth are tired and would prefer to ride instead of walking to Aunt Harriet's and Uncle Simeon's?"

Elizabeth interceded saying, "My dear husband, I would be delighted to walk unless Mattie would rather ride. It's a lovely day and the distance is so short."

Mattie replied, "I would love to walk as well, but Papa, you are spoiling the boy."

"But all children need a bit of spoiling now and then," he replied and suddenly his face clouded with sadness, and he murmured almost under his breath, "How I regret that I didn't spoil you once and a while instead of…" and his voice broke. Immediately Matilda ran over to him, embraced him and said, "Papa, it is all right. Put all the past behind you. I have. Come, your grandson is getting impatient to have his piggyback journey!" Then Amos smiled, and Elizabeth took his hand, and the tall man with the jubilant child on his shoulders, returned to his state of blissfulness

While walking along beside them, Matilda mused about the profound change in her father and the many instances in which he had taken so much pleasure in providing not only his grandson with everything he could imagine any child would ever desire, but Albert and herself as well, with many indulgences and assistance monetarily. He had insisted on sending them on a belated honeymoon to Europe, not only with all expenses paid, but also gave them a generous amount of spending money. He insisted upon running the store for them while they were away, and Elizabeth took care of little Albert and little Amos. After they returned, they found not only the store completely restocked at his expense, but there was a check in the cash box to cover the amount of unpaid accounts of their customers, who had been unable to raise the cash to pay for the provisions they had purchased because of their scanty crops during the previous extremely dry, summer. She enjoyed the excursion to Europe immensely, and all the financial help her father had provided was deeply appreciated. However, what she valued the most was his deep affection for her, his little grandsons, and his fatherly concern for his son-in-law, whom he had previously disapproved. Suddenly Matilda smiled, when realizing just as Elizabeth had previously, that this was indeed the man he had always been submerged somewhere within that once stern exterior, until that day when Harriet visited his office. How grateful I shall always be to her, she mused. Also, she is like a sister to me. Also, I am thankful for Elizabeth, has become the mother I grew up without. Suddenly, her reverie was broken, when her son said "Getty up, Horsey, I want to go faster!" Then before she had a chance to protest that his Grandpa was not a horse and might be weary, the once sternly formal man, quickened his pace, running as though he were a boy himself, while the little boy on his shoulders screamed in delight

After the short, pleasant walk in the balmy spring breezes, with the sun caressing their faces with its warm glances, they arrived at Harriet and Simeon's home, as eager as always, to visit the family they all loved. When approaching the home, they observed Harriet, sitting behind the house in her flower garden shelling peas. She seemed preoccupied, at first, but when she saw them coming, she quickly got up from the the bench and hurried to greet them all with a hug and a kiss. As Elizabeth caressed her daughter's cheek, she noticed that it was wet with tears and her eyes were reddened by much weeping. "My dear girl, whatever is the matter?" she asked.

Matilda, quickly assessing the situation, took little Amos inside the house to visit with Jennie and the younger Elizabeth, who had just waved to them from the kitchen window in order to give her stepmother and father privacy in comforting Harriet, who appeared to be so very sad.

"Oh, I'm sorry," murmured Harriet, attempting to control her sobbing which had returned, as often occurs when one gazes upon loving, sympathetic faces. "I have attempted to control my feelings about this, and usually I can. Also, I can't talk to Simeon about it, because he feels even worse than I do. The last thing I wish for is to burden him. He isn't as quite hearty as he used to be. I didn't mean to ruin your visit. I usually behave in a more mature fashion."

Elizabeth took her sobbing daughter into her arms, kissing her wet cheeks, and then she and Amos took her back to the garden bench, and Amos sat beside her on one side and Elizabeth the other, both with an arm around her. Then Amos, took his spotless, monogrammed handkerchief from his pocket and lovingly wiped away her tears, much in the same manner Harriet had done, as he shed his tears of remorse, when they rode together in his chaise on their way to his reconciliation with Matilda, so many years ago. Afterwards, the couple held Harriet's hand while she shared her sadness about Jennie's plans with them. She managed a smile and said, "Mama, now I know how difficult it was for you when I left New Brunswick to come here! Of course, I was aware of it at that time, but now I believe I am experiencing what you must have felt."

"Yes, My Dearest, I missed you terribly, but that was an entirely different situation. You and Simeon really had no choice but to act as your conscience directed. His folks needed help desperately. Jennie does have a choice and so does Ethan. It doesn't appear from what you have told me, that he is pushing her to go. She seems as eager as he does for the move. And, my dear Harriet, they must make their own decisions about such things, as painful as it is for those who love them and will miss them so much. I am sure that you feel that way as well."

"Indeed, I do, Mama, and I don't understand why I am behaving in this manner," replied Harriet. "I have always attempted to be so strong."

"It is natural for a loving mother to feel as you do, Dearest, and as for 'being strong', you have demonstrated tremendous courage and always have been very stoic." "By the way," Elizabeth added, after gazing at Harriet's weary, pale face, "At what time did you return home after delivering Mary Jenkins baby's last night?"

"Around two a.m.,"

"What time did you arrive there?"

"It was almost three yesterday afternoon. She had a long, very painful labor, and the herbs didn't appear to alleviate her suffering as they usually do for most women whose babies I have delivered."

"My dear girl, you must be exhausted!"

After hearing about the many hours Harriet had spent attending to the suffering young mother, and aware of the extent of her tiredness, Elizabeth realized that this had also contributed to her daughter's tearful state. My poor child, she mused, no wonder she reacted in this manner, instead of her usual stalwart behavior. Tears come much more readily when a person is overtired.

Amos took Harriet's hand gently, and said, "Now it is time for your Papa Amos to intercede. Put that wedding dress material away to use for some other occasion. You, your mother, Jennie, and myself will go to Bangor tomorrow, and I shall purchase a dress for Jennie to wear at her wedding. You already have too much on your shoulders. After that errand is performed, I am going to treat you and Simeon to a little vacation in Boston. Some pampering in a nice hotel and attending some cultural events will provide you with a well deserved respite from all this overworking which you have done for so many years."

"Oh Amos", Elizabeth said, hugging him, "That is just what Harriet needs, and Simeon as well! What a thoughtful and generous husband I have."

"It sounds wonderful, Papa Amos, but so expensive," Harriet replied, leaning over to kiss his cheek. "I don't know if I can accept such a gift. Also, Simeon is so proud, it will be difficult to convince him to do so as well."

"My Dear, the matter is settled. I shall make the arrangements immediately. As your stepfather, I have a right to present you with whatever I please. And, my dear daughter, I owe you more than mere money could ever purchase. I do not even wish to think about how my life was before you came to visit me that day in my office and opened the door to the happiest and most fulfilling life I could have ever imagined."

"But you don't have to repay me for that!"

"I know that, dear Harriet. Anyway, I never could. Now just accept my gift! I have enough trouble with your mother protesting every time I present her with something," he said smiling.

"When you put it that way, how can I resist your generous offer," she said, standing on tiptoes to kiss his cheek. Never have I ever expected to visit Boston! I can't believe that I am really going there! "Then her face clouded with concern as she said, I wonder if I can ever convince Simeon to go? First, it will be difficult to get him to accept your gift, and then he will feel that he is too busy tending the spring crops, and cutting wood to season during the summer so there will be a plentiful supply for winter."

"My dear girl," replied Amos. "Simmy and Jamie can attend to the crops and chores, and I have heard that Peter Jenkins, who recently moved here, needs to earn money to buy livestock and some lumber to build a barn. I shall hire him to do some woodcutting while you and Simeon are away."

"Simeon will never allow you to pay someone to do his work. You know how he feels about taking what he terms as "charity."

"Leave him to me, My Dear. I'm sure that he realizes that a trip like this will do you a world of good, and he will not wish to deprive you of this opportunity for leisure and enjoyment."

When they returned home after their visit with Harriet, Elizabeth embraced her husband gratefully, saying "Amos dearest, you never cease to amaze me! What a wise and generous husband I have. The trip to Boston is just what Harriet needs now. Her life has consisted of mostly work and very little leisure. Also, how you ever convinced Simeon to accept your wonderful gift, fills me with amazement. He has always been so set against accepting anything from anyone, especially an expensive gift such as this trip."

"I simply told him that Harriet desperately needed some rest, which you know my dear, is certainly true. Her weariness is etched in her face. It appears that he has been concerned about it, as well. He agreed to accept my offer, but insisted that he do some work for us in return. I didn't wish to hurt his pride so told him that when he had the time, he could build us one of those beautifully crafted, carved trunks he makes. He said that he would love to, but that it would not be enough repayment. However, he finally agreed to accept our gift of the vacation with his pride at least somewhat intact."

"Oh, I am so thankful that you convinced him to accept your offer of the trip. Harriet will be overwhelmed with joy. Imagine how fascinating it will be for her to see such a sophisticated city such as Boston, after living in this small township for so many years. How she will love the libraries, the concerts, and all those shops, which contain so many beautiful things. But most of all, she won't have to lift a finger to do anything. That will amaze her after working so hard all these years." Then Elizabeth reached up threw her arms around her husband, saying, "I so enjoyed our honeymoon there, My Love!"

"And so did I, my lovely wife! Also, I have basked in joy ever since I met you."

Then the couple held one another's hand, as they headed towards their home, and Elizabeth felt a weight, heavy as a sack of stones, slip away from her shoulders, now that her exhausted daughter would have some much needed leisure and enjoyment.

CHAPTER 25

▼

VACATION

Harriet awakened suddenly, worried that she had overslept, because of the brilliance of the sun dappling the lovely crystal chandelier, which hung from the high ceiling with shimmering diamonds, it appeared to be much later than nine a.m. The first moments after awakening, she visualized herself at home, with all her chores to perform with such a late start. Then, when gazing about the room, Harriet became aware that she was in that lovely hotel room with nothing to do except whatever she might fancy and the household duties at home were being attended to by others. "Oh dear, she whispered to herself, I have never slept so late in my adult life!" While gazing sleepily towards Simeon's side of the bed, she noticed that her husband was not there. He must have gone for a walk she mused. Her early rising husband would never sleep this late! Poor man, he must be ravenous, waiting for me to wake up to join him for breakfast. While the balmy spring breezes flitted through the open window, rustling its rose colored velvet drapes, and filling the room with apple blossom scented air, whose scent drifted in from the large tree just outside the entrance of the building, she washed, using the water provided in the beautiful blue willow patterned pitcher, with its large matching washbowl, and the lovely soap with a scent reminiscent of a garden filled with lavender blossoms. Oh my, she said aloud, "This fluffy face cloth and towel is as soft as goose down. Never have I felt so pampered!" Hurriedly, Harriet donned the lovely new dress, purchased with some of the cash in the envelope labeled "Funds for Fun", which her mother had slipped into her traveling bag while assisting with the packing. After so many years of frugality, she had been reluctant to use the generous gift, which also provided ample funds for more clothing, as well presents to take home for the family. Then, realizing that Mama and Papa Amos would be sad if it remained unspent, Harriet reluctantly utilized the first money she had ever possessed which wasn't needed for necessities. It was as though she were having a beautiful dream and suddenly would awaken to find that she was at home, peering into the little money box in the cupboard where the family funds were kept, to access whether its usual meager supply of coins would be sufficient for their food supply until more money was forthcoming. But of course, all this splendor wasn't an illusion. She was indeed in this lovely room, on a wonderful vacation and must enjoy every moment of Papa Amos's bountiful gift. Harriet waited for a few moments, and since Simeon hadn't returned, she descended the carpeted staircase and found him sitting by a highly polished table, in a high backed cushioned chair, reading the daily newspaper.

While leaning to kiss his cheek, she said, "My Dear, you must be half starved! You should have awakened me."

"My Dear Girl, I couldn't bear to disturb you. You have needed this rest for years," he replied, while gazing at her lovingly.

Even though they had been on vacation in Boston for only three days, the weariness had left Harriet's face and her velvety brown eyes had regained their sparkling beauty. Immediately upon their arrival, she had lamented because she would be loosing time with Jennie, who would be so many miles away from her family in two short months. However, after Simeon had told her how anxious he had been about her exhaustion, and because she was always worried when causing him concern, complied with his wishes for her to enjoy this leisure so kindly provided by her stepfather. Simeon, also, had been reluctant to leave. Not only because of his daughter, whose leaving for Ohio had saddened him as much as it did Harriet, but because, he disliked taking money he hadn't earned from anybody, even from a relative, especially the "spending money." Elizabeth, as she had done with Harriet's, must have slipped it into his valise. Accepting all the funds required for the trip had been difficult for him, but this added generosity, even more so. However, he was delighted now that Harriet was looking so rested and enjoying every place they visited with a childlike joy.

He smiled when reflecting upon her amazement during their visit to the Old North Church, an awesome structure, built in 1723, and constructed with sturdy brick walls, as well as a lofty steeple of 191 feet. She had stood transfixed, while gazing at it, saying "How could anyone ever build anything as high as that steeple? It seems as though its spire brushes the sky."

Later that day they visited a large house which had been a family residence. In 1711, it had burned and in 1718, rebuilt. Later in 1829, the structure had become a printing house as well as a book store, and after the proprietor saw the couple outside observing the structure, he kindly invited them inside to watch the presses. Harriet was as fascinated with them as if she were a small child, as well as being ecstatic with the books which they produced. They carefully selected several tomes, utilizing a portion of Papa Amos's generous gift, to purchase them. Momentarily, while passing the looking glass in the hallway, Simeon gazed at his own countenance, noticing that its tired lines were diminished, which made him feel and appear at least ten years younger.

CHAPTER 26

▼

THE PROBLEM

When Harriet and Simeon returned home, they found that their capable sons and daughters had performed all the necessary chores, gardening, and housework, as proficiently as their parents would have done, had they been there to attend to the duties themselves. Also Peter Jenkins had cut more firewood to season for the winter supply than Simeon would have in that period of time. Jenny was first to dash out to greet her parents, when they arrived with Amos, who had met the couple at the stage station to provide transportation to their home. After she had greeted them with hugs and kisses of welcome, She exclaimed, "Mama! You look as young as you did when I was a little girl! And Papa, so do you! You must have had a wonderful rest and a delightful stay in Boston."

Harriet embraced her daughter, answering, "My Dear, I certainly did! I felt just as though I were a pampered princess! I don't believe that I have ever slept as much as I did there in a whole year's time. What amazing things we saw as well! Also, there were so many folks on the streets. While walking along the sidewalks, I saw a greater number of people than the whole population of Great Pond consists of! And the buildings! Many were built of beautiful brick, with marble pillars and steps at their entrances and the churches' steeple were so lofty that it appeared that they touched the sky! The shops were filled with beautiful china, furniture, clothing, exotic spices, and more lovely things than I could imagine, from many foreign countries. It is still difficult for me to believe that ships can travel such distances to supply such a variety of goods.

Then the reunited family sat around the table enjoying a delicious meal, prepared by Jennie and Elizabeth, consisting of fresh green peas, baby carrots from the garden, a macaroni and cheese casserole, freshly baked bread, a perfectly browned, flaky crusted, rhubarb pie and glasses of tea, cool from the water just drawn from the cold recesses of the well. While savoring the delectable food her girls had prepared, and glancing at the neatly kept house, Harriet smiled, musing about how well they had learned the art of housewifery, feeling quite inevitably, a surge of motherly pride. After they finished the meal and the dishes were cleared away and washed, she took out the gifts she had brought with her from Boston. There was a lovely rose-colored silk dress for Jenny, another one which was brilliant blue, for Elizabeth, her mother's namesake, and a pretty pink, lace trimmed dress for Bethiah. Also, she presented each one of her sons with the first suits they had ever owned, which had not been hand made. Simmie's was navy blue, Jamie's was dark gray, and Joshua's was deep brown. The girls touched the shimmering fabric of their gowns, caressingly, marveling at the luxurious material. Then suddenly Jennie's eyes clouded with sadness, and Harriet immediately responded, "Whatever is the matter, Dearest? Don't you like your new gown?"

"Of course, I think it is the most beautiful garment I have ever seen, but when will I ever get a chance to wear it, after I leave for Ohio?" Then, tears streamed down her cheeks, while thoughts of her separation from her family by so many miles, surged through her being.

"My darling girl," replied Harriet, "I have read that the state has grown considerably, and many places in Ohio have social functions where you will have the opportunity to dress up. Some cities, such as Cincinnati, appear to be quite sophisticated. Also, I have bought some practical cotton dresses and bonnets for your journey, as well as a stout pair of shoes, for your wedding present. I just wanted you to have a nice silk gown as well, but I'm sorry it made you sad." But of course, Harriet was aware that Jennie's tears had not been caused by the suitability of the dress for her use in her future home, but because of the first stirrings of sadness concerning leaving her family as well as everyone else, whom she had grown up with and loved. Her heart ached for her daughter, and she momentarily wondered if Jennie might change her plans and decide not to leave for Ohio after all. But, however tempting was the thought of having her daughter nearby, instead of so many miles away, she was determined to not interfere in any way or utter any opinion on the matter. As determined as Ethan was to make his home in Ohio, if Jennie refused to go, it might result in a serious breach in their relationship, and because of this, she and only she, must make any decisions concerning the move. Harriet, sighed when realizing that the wedding was only a month and a half away. How would she ever find enough time for everything which still needed to be done. Of course if she hadn't spent time away during that trip— Then she smiled, realizing how beneficial it had been not only for her own well being, but for Simeon's as well. Well, she mused, at least the wedding dress is ready, thanks to Papa Amos's generosity. When her mind again returned to the myriad tasks remaining to be performed before the event, she hurried to the kitchen to wash the dishes which she had insisted upon doing, despite her daughter's protests. Somehow, while performing this mindless task, the mere act of immersing her hands in the warm water soothed her, and it seemed as though this mundane chore, was therapeutic. It was almost as though the sudsy liquid momentarily cleansed her psyche of its accumulation of all the worrisome thoughts which surged through it, at least for that brief period of time spent merely attending to a household activity which would be tiresome for most. Just as she finished washing and drying the dishes and started to hang her wet dishcloth and towel upon the little rack beside the kitchen stove, Ethan knocked upon the kitchen door. Harriet attempted to greet him as warmly as she had always done before she had heard about their plans to move to Ohio. However, she was well aware of how her face betrayed her emotions. Even though she had resigned herself to her daughter and future son-in-law's plans, and had made a tremendous effort to convince herself that they had their own lives to live and the right to do so, just as she had done with hers, a few vestiges of resentment lingered towards Ethan because the move was entirely his idea. What is wrong with me? I am not the interfering person my thoughts are compelling me to be. Where is the stoic young woman I was when I left New Brunswick to come here? Then, sighing, she opened the door, managing a warm smile, as well as a hug, as she greeted Ethan. But as she did so, she sensed the uneasiness in his manner which troubled her. Perhaps he realizes that I have been upset about the move, although I have said nothing to him or his family about it, and I am sure that Jennie has respected my wishes not to do so. But suddenly it was apparent to Harriet, that much more than the possibility of her disapproval of the move, was troubling Ethan. His eyes were clouded with concern and his hands were trembling. Whatever could be the matter, she wondered. Then touching his shoulder gently, she asked, "What has happened to upset you so much, Ethan?"

"My brother who moved to Connecticut is very ill and I must go there to assist his wife and five children. He is unable to work and needs my help. The wedding has to be postponed indefinitely, and I just don't know how I can break this news to Jenny."

For a short moment, feelings intermingled with deep concern for Ethan's brother and his family and guilt for the relief which surged through her because her daughter's leaving for Ohio would be postponed, until she observed the anguish etched in Ethan's face. Quickly, she flung her arms around him and murmured comfortingly, "Jennie will be fine, Ethan. She will understand the sad plight of your brother and his family and want you to go to them."

"I know Jennie is a wonderful understanding girl, but do you really think she will not be too disappointed and decide to call the wedding off?"

"Of course she will be disappointed, but she would never perform such a rash and thoughtless act such as calling off the marriage because of circumstances under which you have no control." Harriet gave him another hug and pushed him towards the door saying "Now stop looking so miserable and go tell her."

A few moments later, a much relieved Ethan with his arm encircling Jennie's waist, came out to the garden where Harriet was gathering fresh greens for the evening meal and with his face radiant with love while gazing at his beloved Jennie, said, "Mrs. Wilson, "Could you arrange to have the preacher over tomorrow to marry us quickly? Jenny wants to come with me to help my brother and his family!"

"Of course, I'm sure he would be happy to oblige," she replied, throwing her arms around the couple, saying, "I am so proud of you both and your wisdom and compassion, in putting your own plans aside so cheerfully to attend to the needs of a family who needs your assistance so much."

The next day dawned, sunny, with breezes soft as eiderdown and filled with the fragrance of summer flowerings, whose gentle touch tousled the edges of the veil over the face of the beautiful young bride, dressed like a princess in the lovely silk gown "Grampa Amos," had purchased for her. She stood beside her handsome groom in his Sunday best, while they pledged their vows to one another, and the obliging young minister stood before the them, with a somewhat wistful expression on his face. Perhaps he was hoping that someday he, as well, would be blessed with the kind of happiness which exuded from the faces of this blissful young couple. Gazing at her daughter's radiant face which held not even a hint of disappointment because the wedding which had previously been planned so carefully was replaced by a brief ceremony with only the family attending, and because of the urgency of their mission, there would be no time for the modest honeymoon the couple had planned of an overnight stay in a hotel in Bangor and a tour of the city. Harriet's heart swelled with pride. Also, she felt humbled when comparing how maturely Jennie had dealt with the situation facing her, and how uncharacteristically she had displayed so much of her emotions when hearing of the couple's plans to leave for Ohio to make it their new home. She sighed deeply, musing sometimes, it seems as though one can learn lessons from one's own child. Of course for anyone who knew Harriet well, the perception would be that this instance, was only a brief lapse in the stoic manner in which she had faced difficulties or emotional concerns throughout her life. After refastening a stray pin which had fallen off and had caused a strand of her upswept hairdo to escape, she neatened her hairdo, and went to the kitchen to make a fresh pot of tea While sipping the hot, deep amber liquid, and enjoying its invigorating warmth, she suddenly realized that when her daughter and new husband's postponed journey to Ohio took place at some future date, she would have a more philosophical outlook on the matter. Also, the separation from her oldest daughter, would have already taken place, even though Connecticut, was much nearer home than Ohio. Since the couple had left immediately after the ceremony, there had been no time before for Jenny to inform those who lived out of town of the change in the wedding plans, so Harriet promised to perform this task, to which she promptly attended.

CHAPTER 27

▼

THE LETTER

It does not seem possible that the past two years have passed so quickly, Harriet pondered. Maybe it is because as one grows older time passes more rapidly How could it be 1840 already? So much has changed, she mused, while dragging the heavy braided parlor rug outside for its usual spring airing. Continuing her reverie, she lifted the bulky floor covering over her sturdiest clothesline and proceeded to beat it vigorously to rid it of the accumulation of winter dust. Because this had been one of the chores Jennie had taken on as one of her household tasks, Harriet's thoughts drifted to her daughter, now so many miles away. After spending a year assisting Ethan in caring for his brother, whose health had improved sufficiently at that point to resume the care of his family, the young couple were free to make their journey to Akron, Ohio as they had previously planned. However, they decided to spend a year at home with his family while Ethan worked in the lumber camps during the winter, as well as cutting and selling logs to be sold for railroad ties from the portion of his father's woodlands, which he had given the couple as a wedding present. The funds gleaned from these enterprises, along with a generous monetary wedding gift from Amos, would be used for the trip to Ohio as well as providing money enough to purchase supplies and a modest piece of land for a homestead. Much to Harriet's relief, the couple opted not to make the arduous journey in a covered wagon filled with their possessions. Most of the essentials needed would be purchased upon their arrival. Because of this decision, the couple could travel utilizing stagecoach, steamship, and since the railways were now an accessible mode of transportation, it would be possible for them to complete most of their journey by train. How much more comfortable these conveyances were than having to bump over rough terrain and ford streams in those primitive wagon trains, Harriet mused, and now steamships are traveling from Boston to England! It seems incredible that this young country of ours has progressed so rapidly in such a short span of time!

Smiling, Harriet left the rug outside to continue it's airing, marveling at the rapid pace of progress in not only in traveling, but in such things as more efficient heating provided by the invention of a marvelous stove by Benjamin Franklin which warmed homes so much more effectively, as well as requiring much less wood. When she had finished scrubbing the wide boarded pine floors, she put the kettle on for a pot of tea to enjoy while reading the letter, which had just arrived from Jennie. Her hands trembled with anticipation as she opened the first communication from her daughter. Jenny wrote as follows:

April 2, 1840

Dearest Mama and Papa.

We arrived safely and our journey to Ohio was quite comfortable, except for when the stagecoach got mired with mud almost up to the horses' knees several times along the way. Poor creatures! I felt so sorry for them, but we all got off the coach and walked alongside until the going got better. The steamship was lovely and I can't believe how nice its furnishings were. I felt quite pampered while aboard. The train was a marvel, zipping along its tracks at about 20 miles an hour! All those wonderful inventions have made traveling so much easier.

I could hardly believe our good fortune, when Ethan and I had the opportunity to purchase a two story house and 50 acres of land just four days after we arrived here! When we went to the land agent's office to inquire about acquiring a few acres, we met a young couple, Mr. And Mrs. Perkins, who were returning to Boston because they were homesick, and wished to dispose of their property so that they could return to Boston and get resettled before winter. With the money from "Grandpa" Amos and Papa Collins for our wedding presents, along with money Ethan had saved, we had not only enough to purchase the property, but some left for supplies. How wonderful it is not to have to build a house before winter! All we have to do is to complete the finishing off of the interior! Also, there is some furniture! The Perkins's didn't want to be burdened with taking it with them, so we now have a comfortable bedstead with a feather stuffed mattress, a set of drawers, a kitchen table, and four chairs, as well as a settee for what will become our parlor. I can't believe our good fortune! There is even a Franklin stove, so we shall be warm and cozy during the winter. Not only do we have the luxury of enough furnishings to make us comfortable, but they just gave them to us! With the lovely braided parlor rug you made for our wedding present placed upon the floor and the linens I brought with me already put to use, our little "nest" seems quite like home.

I'm happy that we decided to settle in Akron. Since the Erie Canal was completed, this place has really flourished. We have the benefit of all sorts of goods, food staples, and even sugar, as well as coffee and tea. We never expected to have such things available to us at our arrival. We really imaged more primitive conditions. Also, a lovely little schoolhouse has just been built in Akron, which is just five miles from where our homestead is. It will be wonderful to have a place of learning so close to us when we are blessed with children!

We miss you all very much, but are so excited and happy with our new life here, and hope, dear Mama and Papa, that you will share our joy in this place we have chosen to make our home. I must close for now, because I must start a stew for supper. How I have rambled on!

Much love to all and many hugs and kisses.

Your devoted daughter, Jenny

Tears spattered the pages while Harriet read the long awaited letter, although when learning that her daughter and son-in-law had arrived at their destination safely, relief surged through her being such as one feels when a tumultuous storm has abated. Also, she felt comforted to learn that the young couple would have the comfort of an already existing house rather than having to construct one before the approach of winter and that there was enough furniture to set up housekeeping as well as a nice stove to keep them cozy. Harriet took out her handkerchief, wiped away her tears and smiled, feeling much less sad about her daughter's leaving to make her home so many miles away. Then she took the letter out to the barn where Simeon was doing the milking, because she was too eager to share the good news concerning their daughter, rather wait for him to complete his chores. Immediately after the anxious father had read his daughter's letter, it would be shared with the other family members.

CHAPTER 28

▼

REFLECTIONS

Harriet sat in her favorite chair, dreamily watching the crimson-gold flames prancing over the beech logs in the fireplace. This simple mode of relaxation always seemed to fill her with contentment and a feeling of well being. Outside, the wind dashed icy snowflakes against the window panes, but despite the storm, the pleasant aroma of the mince pie she had baked for supper still lingered in the room, and along with warmth of the fire, she felt snug and cozy. As usual, her hands were occupied with a needlework project while she sat in her cushioned rocking chair beside the hearth, and this one was a christening dress for Jennie's first child, her namesake, Harriet. How relieved she had been when her daughter's letter had arrived, announcing the birth of a healthy baby girl, whose birth had been an easy one. The thankful, happy, grandmother held up the long, white linen garment, making certain that every stitch was perfect. When it passed her careful inspection, she took out the delicately tatted trim she had produced during the previous week and attached it to the gown. Just as Harriet carefully placed the little dress in a box to send to her daughter, twelve year old Bethiah came into the room carrying two flannel nightgowns she just finished making for her tiny niece.

Harriet looked up from her work, saying, "My dear child, what beautiful little gowns these are! Your sewing rivals that of a professional seamstress. I am so proud of you, Love, although I am wondering why you are so are up so late."

"I am glad that you like my work, Mama. I didn't want to go to bed until the nightgowns were finished, because I knew you were planning to send out the parcel soon."

Harriet hugged her industrious child, her heart filled with motherly pride. How much she resembles her grandmother, not only in her helpfulness and kindly nature, but she looks just like I would have pictured Bethiah would have when she was the same age as her little namesake. What a joy and comfort my little girl is to me, just as that dear, motherly women was to me. Just then, a sunbeam illuminated the parlor window, filtering through the lace curtains Bethiah had made, and it seemed as though, momentarily, that Harriet sensed her presence. A sensation of warmth and comfort permeated her being, such as she had experienced when arriving, shivering and hungry that stormy evening, after the long journey from New Brunswick, and her mother in law had draped a warm shawl around her shoulders while she ate the hot, delicious stew which she had prepared for the weary travelers. After tucking the young Bethiah into bed, and finishing the preparation of the parcel for Jennie, Harriet slipped quietly into bedroom, so not to awaken Simeon, while that loving, comforting awareness she had experienced yet lingered.

The next morning Harriet remained in a reflective mood It seemed impossible to her that 21 years had elapsed since she and Simeon made their trip by ox-cart from New Brunswick to Great Pond. Time seemed to pass as rapidly as water poured through a sieve. She found it difficult to believe that two years had elapsed since Jenny and Ethan had left to make their home in Akron, Ohio. Her little namesake was already one year old. Jenny's most recent letter's first lines were: "Little Harriet is beginning to look a lot like you, Mama. Her hair is quite abundant, and it is the same red-gold shade as yours, although I believe that she will be much taller than you are because she is already quite tall for her age. I believe that her height probably comes from Ethan's side of the family, because his sisters are both over five feet five. She is strong and healthy and took her first step yesterday, so will be walking soon." Three weeks later, a small parcel containing a daguerreotype of little Harriet arrived from Jennie and her delighted grandmother touched her lips against the tiny likeness of her beloved granddaughter.

The yearning to see her grandchild as well as the daughter whom she missed so much was sometimes overwhelming. More comfortable and speedier transportation added to Harriet's temptation to make the journey, but Simeon's health was a consideration at this point. The rheumatism in his knees caused him a great deal of pain and recently, he had a chest cold, which was of such long endurance that Harriet was afraid it might have resulted in pneumonia. After Simeon recovered from that affliction, he appeared to be extremely tired and had lost much of his energy. Under no circumstances, despite her longing to visit Jennie and her little Harriet, could she leave her beloved husband while he was in this state of health, and he certainly didn't possess the energy to accompany her on a journey of such considerable distance. Harriet was grateful that Simmy and Jamie were there to take responsibility for all the chores and farm work which required the most arduous labor. Also, Lucinda, Simmy's wife, whom she loved as a daughter, along with Elizabeth and Bethiah, were of tremendous assistance in lightening her own workload, by taking upon themselves many tasks which Harriet had performed previously. Because of their help, she had a great deal of time to spend on her own projects, especially such things as her little compositions for her clavichord, and her "dabbling" in watercolors and poetry. After so many years of feeling twinges of guilt about her few "stolen" moments away from her numerous duties, it seemed such a luxury to have time for herself. If she had to choose among these three artistic pursuits, it would her painting, because somehow, it transported her into another realm, whose mysterious space could not be permeated by any cares or problems she might be experiencing. Her music and poetry did much the same, but her watercolors gave her opportunity to spend time absorbing the essence of each tiny bloom, a bird perched atop a rock preening itself, her flower garden, or the myriad other pastoral scenes she loved so much. Also, her paintings where usually done outside with the sun caressing her face and the soul stirring peace which she always experienced when basking in the delightful splendors of nature permeated her soul. Although she had always experienced this ecstasy when basking in its beauty, she could now do so without concern for whatever obligations might be awaiting her attention, because of the loving assistance of her daughters and Lucinda. During all the years, which had required so much of her time and energy, it had been almost impossible to imagine so much time for leisure. Yes, Harriet mused, I have a wonderful life and have been richly blessed with a loving family and good friends. Tonight would be a special one, because Amos and Elizabeth, as well as Albert, Matilda, Albert Jr. and Amos 11 would be arriving to share the evening meal. Later in the evening, Jonathan, Amy, Ben, and Susan had planned to join them after their own guests had left. How much larger the family circle has grown during these past 21 years, Harriet marveled. Then suddenly aware that she must set the yeast dough to rise for rolls for supper, she smiled contentedly and rushed to the kitchen to perform this task. While kneading the dough, she contemplated on how thankful she was for the blessings which had bestowed upon her during the past forty-one years of her life, and a blissful surge of contentment permeated her being.

Bibliography

Archer, Gleason L. LL.D, A Great-Great-Grandson. Ancestors and Descendants of Joshua Williams: A Mayflower Descendant & Pioneer. Boston. Wright & Potter Printing Co. 1927.

Compendium of Cookery and Reliable Recipes: Two Complete Volumes in One. Containing The Entire Compilation of Rules for Cooking and Confectionary, Together With The Book of Knowledge, or 1000 Ways of Getting Rich, As Compiled by Mrs. E. C. Blakeslee of Chicago, Miss Emily Leslie of Philadelphia, and Dr. S. H. Hughes, Chemist of Boston, Rev., Enlarged, and Illustrated. Chicago. The Merchants' Specialty Co., Pub. 1890.

Crawford, Mary Caroline Social Life In Old New England Little Brown & Co.1914.

Everyday Life in The 1800's: A Guide For Writers, Students & Historians. McCutcheon, Marc, ed. Writer's Digest Books. Cincinnati, Ohio. C1993.

New England. Text by Susi Forbes. Produced by David Gibbon. Crescent Books. 1985

New England Wilds: The American Wilderness. Tanner, Ogden and The Editors.of Time-Life Books. New York. Time-Life Books. 1979 Reprint.

Nylander, Jane C. Our Own Snug Fireside: Images of the New England Home 1760-1860. Knopf. Distributed by Random House. C1993.

Rich, Louise Dickinson. The Coast of Maine: An Informal History and Guide. Camden, Maine. Down East Books (Reprint. 1995 (Arrangement with Harper Collins Pubs. Inc. 1995.)

Smith, Marion Jacques A History of Maine From Wilderness to Statehood. Falmouth Publishing House. Portland, Maine. 1949.

Trollope, Mrs. Frances. Domestic Manners of the Americans. New York. Alfred A. Knopf. 1949.

Wirth, Fremont P. United States History. American Book Co. 1949.

World Almanac. Commemorative Ed. (The Complete 1868 Original & Selections From 25, 50, and 100 Years Ago, with an Overview by Today's Editors.) Edited by June Foley, Mark Hoffman, & Tom McGuire. New York. Pharos Books. A Scripps Howard Co. c1992.

0-595-28792-1